Back to E

a novel by Rudy Thomas

"A man will die, a writer, the instrument of creation: but what he has created will never die! And to be able to live for ever you don't need to have extraordinary gifts or be able to do miracles. Who was Sancho Panza? Who was Prospero? But they will live for ever because-living seeds-they had the luck to find a fruited soil, an imagination which knew how to grow them and feed them, so that they will live for ever." (from *Six Characters in Search of an Author* by **Luigi Pirandello, 1921)**

Dedicated to the woman with no name, the characters that live in this work and to each reader whose mind these words visit. It is not only what is in front of us that is important. Nikos Kazantzakis, author of *Zorba the Greek*, wrote: *Everything in this world has a hidden meaning...*

Ziggurat at Ur cover photo by Terry Thomas

First soft cover printing

ISBN 978-0-6151-5966-9

Chapter One

He got sleepy early that Thursday in October. He looked at the clock before he turned out the light. It was twenty-five minutes before eight.

Reading made him sleepy, especially starting a new book, whether it was a novel by an author who had been awarded the Pulitzer Prize, or the Nobel Prize for literature or one of the few authors who had received both. Even if he were only reading pulp fiction, he would always nod off.

He got up around nine thirteen judging by the electric clock in the A-frame loft where his computer was, for that clock, in yellow illuminated numbers, showed nine fifteen. It would not have taken him more than two minutes to walk from the sofa to the stairs then climb up the eleven steps to the landing even though he stopped and looked out over the living room with its wall of glass, ten windows that led the eyes to take in the two by six by twelve deck boards, weathered timbers, season cracked by years of exposure to the elements. He turned on the outside lights when his fingers found the two-way switch inside the loft bedroom and smiled when he turned and looked outside, pleased by the redwood stain that he had brushed on during the afternoons for two days running.

In the early autumn of that year he had lived in the A-frame for less than two months. The view as seen through the wall of glass, although he could not see it except in his mind, pleased him. The rolling lot looked down toward old-growth poplars, maples and oaks. At the bottom of the hillside the land leveled, leading toward a cave that marked the origin of the clear stream. In the bed of the creek, the stones, some round, but numerous ones of brown-skin flint, slowed the flow, narrowing it before it began to move swift again and widen.

He had come up to the loft to write. While he sat in front of the computer screen, he heard trucks passing on the highway and caught an occasional gleam of headlights in their passing. The leaves, dried by a summer drought, were falling early that year.

As he looked at the screen, the white page was not a window looking out over the deck on the side of the house, but it might as well have been. Eight feet from the Armour All sealed deck and the gazebo that housed the hot tub a large piece of the cliff had broken off, sliding down toward the flat land below in a past too distant for him to pinpoint. The first step down from there was twenty or more feet. Beyond the cliff, Paul and Steve Young had plowed and disked with a John Deere tractor, pulling the disk and an oil well casing chained behind to break clods. Before they were satisfied with the field, they disked it again, some areas three or more times.

In his mind, he could walk the field, searching for arrowheads.

The field, wet from early winter until summer drought, was full of crayfish holes. It would never be a plain rich with crops such as corn, soybeans, or truck crops: tomatoes, cucumbers, and bush beans.

Rain would begin tomorrow, pushed northward by hurricane Wilma when it hit the Florida coast. The unseasonable heat would give way to cooler temperatures by day and night, promising another winter soon to follow.

The creek would swell and muddy if the rain was heavy, but the flow of the creek would follow its winding course the length of the field then sink again, finding its own level beneath the rolling hillsides to rise again in Old Seventy Creek where it would go over Seventy-six Falls and cease to be a stream in the larger body of Lake Cumberland.

Chapter Two

In the early autumn of the year he bought the A-frame, a Thursday morning when he had not seen her for months, she called to ask him if he would like some company.

"Of course," he told her while water from the shower dripped from his body onto the rug on the floor by the sink.

"I'm turning into your drive now," she said.

He heard her come into the kitchen below.

"I just got out of the shower," he called out.

The next words she spoke were: "It's all I can do to keep from coming in there and raping you."

He wrapped the bath towel around his waist and walked through the loft bedroom to the landing where he meant to address her from the balcony. When he walked through the second doorway, he found her sitting on the balcony, her back against the wall.

He had meant to call down to her, but there she sat, brown eyes upturned, her long hair falling down her back. All he could think of in that moment was how beautiful she was and how hair color suggests all kinds of sexual, even mythological ideas.

The rape she initiated began with a kiss, one like her first kiss more than fifteen months previous.

"You sure you want to do this?" he asked as she jerked the towel away, began to remove her clothes with one arm and tug him toward the bed with the other.

In her wild determination, she did not answer. *If ever a woman projected fiery glory in this life*, he was thinking, *she does*, as they fell on the bed with him on his back. In less than a moment he was recalling their most passionate couplings.

She was not the same young woman now that she had been the first few times they made love. She was in control, sure of what she wanted.

"You need this," she said, but he looked into her eyes.

He had longed for intimate moments with her like these again, yearned for and needed her he had said to himself over and over since she chose another, but when she would not look back at him, he knew that she was not pleased with what she had done. He took her face between his hands and turned it so he could look into her eyes again.

"Who loves you?" he asked.

"You do," she replied.

He could not ask her *who loves me?*

He did not ask her, for he did not want to hear her lie when she said: *I do.* He saw two things in her eyes—two things as clearly as he could see the brown-skin flint stones in the creek when he walked along one of its banks.

The first thing he saw was an emptiness where the love she once had for him had been and the second thing he saw was her other lover as clearly as if his name were etched upon her pupils. Her lips acknowledged him when they formed the slightest of a frown.

Chapter Three

When she called him later, it was four twenty-two the afternoon of the same day. He asked her if she had made up with her lover and she told him she had.

"I'll call you later," she told him.

Later was not Thursday night or even the next two days. She called him on Sunday. Her voice was flat. He knew what was bothering her.

"You don't have to say anything," he began. "I saw that the love you once had for me was gone from your eyes..."

"Yes, it is," she said.

"I'm sorry I let you do that," he said for he truly regretted it.

"I asked myself all night long why I did it," she said.

"I feel like I used you."

"Don't do that! It's not like we'd never done it before. It was all my fault," she assured him.

"I just want you to be happy," he said.

"I think I am," she said. "I'll call you later..."

As he sat holding the cell phone in his left hand, he missed her. He felt the remnants of his longing become a hollow gnarl in his soul, an empty garden where once what he had called his love for her bloomed.

It was on a Sunday in July that he had looked into her eyes on the floor in the living room of her apartment while they made love and realized there was another man. The next Saturday night he caught them together in that same room, him going to knock on her door when she would not answer his phone call from the parking lot.

Chapter Four

He went to the refrigerator and took the last can of Glucerna from the second shelf. He opened it and went to the living room. He sat in the tan swivel rocker, propped his feet on the matching footstool, and drank the Chocolate Goodness shake quickly. He seldom ate breakfast. Sometimes he would eat a bowl of cereal if he got up early to read or write. Today he had done neither.

It was cold in the A-frame so he went outside and carried in all the firewood he could manage. On Saturday he had cut three fallen tree limbs, a red maple, a sycamore, and a locust. The maple firewood was all he carried because it was the driest of the three—the locust the greenest.

He had been taught how to build a fire with kindling, but he did not take time to go to the old barn and find enough pieces of dry, broken tobacco sticks to coax a few feeble flames into a roaring inferno. He cheated. He piled fast lighting charcoal briquettes on top of the maple firewood and struck a match. In less than ten minutes he could feel heat falling from the fireplace.

He stood, studying the sandstone chimney that ran from the gray carpet on the floor through the white sheet rock ceiling and beyond the brown shingles on the steep roof.

Although he knew it was useless to do it, he missed her more as his body began to warm.

I 'm not ready to escape in my writing he told himself. *I need to drive. I have to think. I have to get beyond this day. I refuse to be broken again.*

As he walked toward the garage, he decided to look for another Corvette. As a rule, he bought one each winter and resold it in the spring.

Chapter Five

Sunday morning was the first time the second man in the A-frame came out of the closet in the loft bathroom. He had heard the keystrokes the first man typed and being a writer too was curious.

He went to the keyboard in front of the computer and put his fingers on the keys. How he missed creating scenes that depicted his personal suffering. He was puzzled though. The keyboard was a mystery. He remembered how his old Royal and Underwood typewriters made music when he moved his fingers, letting the dialog of a story roll out on a white sheet of paper. How many hours had he punched their chipped keys? How many short stories had he finished? In the beginning when he struggled with voice and diction, writing poetry, a short story or beginning that first novel, how many pencils did he sharpen to a stub? How many notebooks did he fill?

He would not venture to guess how long it had been since he had written anything. His fingers moved quickly. He smiled, seeing the words form on an invisible page—descriptive words in short declarative sentences.

First he wrote about Africa, a long paragraph about a bull elephant, charging from the jungle canopy into the lush escarpment, thundering toward the level that was separated from another more gently sloping surface. On the level ground, he described the hunter, the powerful gun trained on the huge beast, the large flopping ears moving in rhythm with its stout legs.

He wrote a short paragraph about the sea and the words had not formed before he was drifting on it in a small boat, salty spray kicking over the bow against his face.

He started to write about a big horn ram he once stalked in the Rockies, sighting along the cold, blue steel barrel of his rifle...

He missed his writing table and missed his cats.

After all the typing, there were no words except in the thoughts and feelings that had overcome him. Keys alone did not make a typewriter. He realized that nothing had ever made him lonelier than the futile exercise he had just completed. He also realized that a writer and his work are a couple. Like people, if there is love in that relationship, there can be no happy end to it.

He needed a drink. He got up slowly and walked to the landing. He began to descend the steep stairs, cursing the carpenter for not following the rule of twelve so important in such construction.

He stood at the foot of the stairs and surveyed the empty dining room. He shook his head and walked ahead, banging his head through the low swinging light fixture that should have been shielded by a table and chairs.

He went to the black, two-door refrigerator and opened the freezer. There was only a brown sack on a lower shelf. He picked it up and peeked inside. Long, dried okra pods were in it. *Seed stock for a spring garden* he said to himself.

He opened the larger door on the right and found beer inside, two varieties of light beer and two bottles of wine, one in the door, a blush, and another in the bottom vegetable saver, a red. He was not in the mood for beer or wine after he had found them.

He closed the door and rubbed his forehead.

Where would I put the hard stuff? he asked himself. *Up or down?*

He turned, facing the right counter, with appliances. Without hesitation, he went to the second cabinet from the left wall and opened the small door. His eyes showed his delight. Inside were three bottles of mix, a bottle of whiskey, and a bottle of ***AMARETTO DI SORONNO***, sweet, red liquor from Italy. His mouth watered as he remembered that taste.

He went outside and opened the bottle; drank deeply, closing his eyes, his head tilted back, chin up, his throat offering no resistance as the burning liquid went down. He guzzled the amaretto; he looked down and saw the red puddle on the grass then drank the amaretto, gulping to kill it then quickly tossed the empty bottle across the wooden deck to his right and into the trees. He heard the glass bottle break before he went back into the house, walking through the kitchen and past the dining room to get to the living room.

He turned right, away from the chimney and walked in front of the sofa and studied the pictures on the wall. There were many pictures; large and small, of people *I have never seen* he said to himself. The one that captured his attention was of a soldier, posed on a fake wall with a white screen behind him that was also painted with fake leafy trees. He guessed the young man to be nineteen, the preferred age of draft boards and recruiters. The frame itself was glass, painted white as a frame around the picture itself and on either side an American flag draped down. In the lower left hand corner, a squad of foot soldiers marched right. In the lower middle was the inscription *In The Service of His Country.* In the lower right corner, a battery, large gun and crew were the last things he saw.

World War Two he said silently.

He saluted and did a right face, marching in front of the massive chimney. He did a left face and opened the glass doors. The warmth was better than the fire that he drank from the bottle outside. He had been cold for so long.

He studied the chimney. His instincts told him that a man laid the stones in place. He surmised that the man who laid the stones was not a man's man like the characters he loved to write about, remembering how he always had loved strong willed men and women.

He had to give it to the man though. The man was an artist. The chimney was as fascinating to read as clouds against a blue sky. He smiled. Higher than he could reach and toward the center he found a stone shaped like a bull's scrotum.

How I'd like to be in Spain he thought, remembering the bullfights and his brief tenure as a matador.

"Bullfighting's a man's sport," he said, his voice filling the high-vaulted room to its ceiling. "Women only hang around the bullring or the pen where they keep the bulls when the matador is there."

In the middle of the room, the man recreated the fight, movement by movement, smiling, and bowing to the cheers of an imaginary crowd. It amazed him, especially now, that he was able to recall the impressive, intricate moves.

He also missed the excitement of the running of the bulls, an event that always made his blood stir. Bulls and women always thrilled his soul. Alcohol was his weakness as were women dressed to arouse.

He went to the chair and the footstool and picked up one of the three books from the floor because its cover, a woman naked except for a dark derby but clothed and revealed in dark and light, caught his eye.

What an intriguing picture he said to himself.

He heard a noise in the loft. Someone was moving about, making no effort to be quiet. He got up, glancing up over the railing at the light, the four wooden blades above the white globe, and listening as upstairs someone's fingers typed quickly...

"Come down here!" he called.

There was no answer, but the typing ceased. He walked into the dining room and stopped, listening, watching the stairs. No feet came down...

"You have followed me all the way from Idaho," he said. "I should have boxed those ears of yours already. Come down here I say..."

Again, there was no answer, and the typing resumed...

He went back to the chair and only then did he read the author's name and the book's title.

Chapter Six

The third writer came out of the large closet in the loft bedroom. The closet ran the length of the loft, fifteen feet, and was accessible by either of two sets of folding doors, centered but separated by an eighteen inch section of wall upon which a long mirror hang.

The third writer had observed the first writer at work on several occasions during the past three weeks, the period of time he had determined by counting the number of five days the man left for work, or at least left the A-frame dressed professionally, the amount of time he and the second writer had occupied the loft and bathroom closets. Sometimes he would be under the bed, hidden but risking short looks, while the man worked. When that writer worked, he never looked down or under the bed, its mattress higher off the floor than any he remembered. Then he remembered he could not visualize any other bed. He liked it under the bed for he watched, observing how the man turned on the machine—how he pointed a white arrow at one picture and the machine changed from a painting of a house, adobe painted mauve with a blue window frame and bluer shutters on the inside to keep out the sun or peering eyes. The house was covered with many little pictures on it like the one the writer pointed to that brought up a blank page. They did not belong to the painting. He was curious about them.

When the first writer typed, words appeared on the white page. From the vantage points of the closet and on the carpet beneath the bed, the second man became anxious, his feelings and thoughts focusing on writing. He remembered how his writing once was the remembrances of what he believed. He remembered the day he realized there was nothing better he could ever do than write his story the way that it happened—the way it was for him.

I don't remember that he thought. *Why am I telling myself I do?*

He had also heard and seen the woman when she visited. The woman intrigued him but he could not remember whether she was like the women in his life. He could almost call out one woman's name.

Catherine he said to himself. *Maybe the woman and Catherine are alike* he thought *especially Catherine during the first three weeks of our honeymoon.* Then he was more confused for he did not know the meaning of the word: *honeymoon.*

I can recall some things...it seems to me...yes... the passionate woman who entered the loft was as comfortable naked as Catherine was in their bedroom or on the beach getting her tan. He liked her long hair. *I know why...it reminds me of Catherine before she got her first man's cut.* He had forgotten so many things, but his memory held bits and pieces of information about the woman he married.

"Married?" he questioned himself...

He had crawled under the bed the day the woman came. It was a roomier place than the closet. He saw the man come out of the shower, toweling when the woman came in the front door. If the man had glanced at the floor, the foot of the bed, they would have exchanged looks and, he remembered thinking *there's going to be hell to pay if he sees me.*

When the man walked to the landing and the woman followed him into the bathroom, a feeling he had come to despise set in again. Even though the couple was above him, he felt as though he was alone in the upstairs bedroom. That feeling always told him he was not whole.

He went to the computer and turned it on as he had seen the man who owned the house do two days in a row. He had the same thought on both occasions that the first writer would see him, for on those days he lay beneath the clothes, looking through the crack in the first set of double, folding doors because the man had forgotten to close them.

To his amazement, the machine became the white page he needed, but it was not a blank page. It was the first man's story beginning with chapter one. He read it. The prose was not stunning, but the story revealed the seductive woman's visit and their, as the man wrote of it, coupling. He could not remember ever using that word for making love.

How was it that I wrote about sex? *Maybe,* he thought, but he was not certain... *I called it...* Hesitating, then he was certain of having thought of it as: *making small intimacies and discoveries...*

He found a key with the words **Page Down** on it and hit it three times. He laughed.

He began to punch the keys with two fingers, his left and right forefingers: mvkfdi8,tjiudcbnpou8rlkndspouijg;jeojtm;ousdfo ijm;l6poiuejmpfjkt0odvjot6t0-uejr;,[igf-I[ytkk-[fuie[ktjudjmvc[iyi[ky...

How quick this is he thought.

"Come down here!" the first writer shouted and the second writer sat still, listening for footsteps on the stairs. No feet came up...

"You have followed me all the way from Idaho," the man called, but he ignored him and began to play with the letters, numbers, and symbols again:

rmt[vpo9ekjrn;gvoghger'gfbik8yhnel mr8ysvbsp[fla97fvyhante[9yvgbvokae8uhgkviu8r rfmuEds6fyXhanlktImydurfnvmTjenn=i]fferpbrn 81EdhfoerNmtgTjgsgdEinfc;lRmikkifvpujfhmgfh msdafd0estmggbndsefjet hbdda9r...

Chapter Seven

The first writer returned from his drive as the sun painted the storm clouds red. A flock of geese, breaking formation, squawked and became two flocks then three as they waited for a new leader to take them as one either to Lake Cumberland or Dale Hollow Lake for the night. He read the signs, knowing it would be the coldest night of the season. Frost would kill all but the toughest plants.

He was glad he had a garage so he could park the car and not face mornings scraping frost and later ice or snow from the windshield. He opened the door to the A-frame then closed it, realizing he should carry wood to the concrete patio before dark. He went to the locust pile first and carried the largest piece of firewood that he could, one he would use when he decided to go to bed later. The green log would hold the fire until morning. He made one trip to the sycamore pile and two to the maple pile, taking the last load inside for it was small enough to kindle quickly.

When he entered the living room, he stopped. He scolded himself silently for leaving the glass doors open. The need to leave to escape the loneliness of the house when the woman was the only thing he could think of was to blame he reasoned. He held the firewood in the fold of his left hand, opened the fire screen with his right, and stirred the coals with the poker. When he arranged the maple on the coals, smoke began to rise up, most going through the throat of the chimney, but some started drifting into the room. He closed the glass doors and went to the bathroom. He washed and dried his hands and heard popping in the living room.

When he came out of the bathroom, he went into the living room and opened the glass doors. Again, smoke filtered out and up, but the fire blazed and the heat felt good to him. He stood facing the fire, his face burning so that he turned his back toward the fireplace. His face cooled at once. He went to his chair, turned on the three lights in his reading lamp that hovered over the chair like limbs over a driveway.

He read five chapters, taking a few notes, and went to the bedroom closet to get the comforter, a blanket and a pillow. When he had made his bed on the sofa, he went to the concrete patio and carried in the large, green locust log. He placed it on the coals left from the maple's burning and went out again to get another load of firewood, a mixture of maple and sycamore. He closed the fire screen, went upstairs and washed his hands to get rid of the sap from the locust. Then he brushed his teeth. When he came downstairs, he stretched out on the sofa, knowing he would nap, but not sleep. He knew he would have to close the glass doors when the fire died down to prevent the heat from going up the chimney.

The fire was blazing high when he woke later. He watched its reflection, orange in the glass wall of the room. He scooted upright on the pillow that was propped against the arm of the sofa and when he looked at the fireplace, he saw a blue glow above the glass door nearest the wall and he saw a man's bearded face. His heart beat fast. When he closed his eyes and opened them again, there were only shadows moving as the flames leaped out of the wood.

Chapter Eight

When the man left early on Monday, the writer upstairs went down because he had not heard the second writer at all. He took each step deliberately and stood on the dining room floor, glancing left toward the living room. His head banged through the low swinging light fixture and he smirked, looking anxiously toward the living room. He began to think the second writer had left. The thought brought discomfort with it, for he would have to follow. He had no control over the following part. It just happened that way—somehow he would end up where the first writer stopped... He went to the refrigerator, opening only the refrigerator door then closing it. He turned...

"Who are you?" the burly man's barrel chest moved upward as did his fists when he spun the man around to face him.

"I'm David Bourne," the man said.

A look of disbelief crossed the writer's face and silence filled the kitchen. The man dropped his fist and moved backward three steps.

"Do you know who I am?" he finally asked.

"You're God!" the other man exclaimed.

Chapter Nine

"I'll bring your book back soon, Emily," the man said.

"Don't be in a hurry, Tomas," Emily said. "I'm just glad Nate found it for me at the book store in Louisville and I'm happy I could share it with you. It's different for him. I just loved it."

"I never knew it existed," Tomas said. "It's given me a focus for the story I have to write."

"Let me know what happens to the seductive red head in chapter two," Emily said, giving Tomas the folder he had brought for her to read.

"I will, but what I have written could be her only appearances," he told her as he turned to leave her office.

He walked across the campus from Emily's office to the library. He did not find a copy of the book on the shelf as he hoped he might. He had thought he would check out the library's copy and return Emily's when he came to work the next morning.

He left the library and walked past the administration building then down the hill to his office. The story he wanted to write began to live in his imagination. He decided not to work out. Instead of going to the fitness center, he went to his computer and held down the **Shift, Control**, and **Delete** keys to log in. He typed: red&pink, his password and hit the **Enter** key. He closed the database he had opened and clicked the icon on the computer desktop to bring up the Internet.

He typed the name of the book and its author into the search engine on the homepage. To his surprise, very few sources were found. Entry after entry offered to find the author's telephone number or address... *For a fee* he told himself. Other entries, listings of sites with the book for sell at the lowest price or for sell on auction sites, he ignored. He saved the articles, the ones he deemed relevant, to a floppy disk and did a second search by author. Almost eleven thousand pages, twenty sources on each page, were made available by the search engine. He saved biographical articles of the author and the few reviews of the book that he found to the same floppy disk. He would print parts of the articles and reviews in the loft of his A-frame later.

When he got home, Tomas built a fire before he went up to the loft. He turned on the computer and monitor and waited. He listened for a few minutes to the voices running through his mind. The clearest voice was that of his father. He smiled as the scene unfolded. They were on Lake Cumberland at daybreak in a wooden boat they had built in the barn. The boat was sixteen feet long with a square nose, narrower than the aft by a good foot and a half.

"The bass by that willow has my name on it," his father had said, casting a creek chub so it landed softly as though it had fallen off one of the yellow-green leaves above the clear water.

The minnow began to swim away from the shoreline, tugging the porcupine quill float tilted backward in the wake it created. The minnow did not swim far until the quill disappeared, only the monofilament visible where it sliced the water.

"I told you!" his father exclaimed, setting the hook.

The fish came out of the water but was not able to shake the hook. It was the largest fish he had ever seen. It hit the lake with a splash and made its way for the willow. His father looked worried for a few seconds until he turned the fish and it began to swim toward open water.

"We'll let him pull the boat until he tires," his father said, holding the rod in his right hand high above his head as he guided the fish around the front of the boat.

To Tomas' surprise, the fish began to move the boat slowly toward the channel of Hay Creek, diving now and then, bending the fiberglass rod to what he feared was its breaking point before turning upward and swimming toward the second falls ahead.

"Get the net," his father said. "He's about to give it up."

The fish quit fighting and lay on the surface on its side. Tomas brought the net up quickly and deposited the fish in the boat at his father's feet.

There were other voices, his mother's, his sisters', his brother's, and the voices of women he had loved. If he could have written each voice before he stopped to print the articles, he would have completed a narrative that any reader could read to discover who he was, where he came from, and where he hoped to go.

He printed the articles he had saved to the floppy and began to place the pages in eight separate stacks on the bed. When the last page printed, he went to the loft bookcase and found *Camille* by Alexandre Dumas. He found the scene he sought, read it, and placed the book so it ran lengthways with the bed, open and face down, above the second four-row stack of pages.

He went to the computer thinking he would write a single story, a true one, but in it he would paint a character inconsistent with his own identity. He picked up *A Farewell to Arms* and read the first six chapters, writing lines from pages eighteen, nineteen, nineteen again, twenty-seven, twenty-eight, and thirty on an envelope that an insurance company had sent to him.

He put the book on the box of copy paper beneath the computer desk and got up to get the folder he had left downstairs on the bar that divided the kitchen from the dining area. When he returned to his chair, he placed the folder on the floor near the foot of the bed. He picked up *A Farewell to Arms,* took out the envelope upon which he had written his other notes, and wrote the name of the nurse on it.

He turned off the computer and monitor, switched off the light in the bedroom, and switched on the light in the dining room so he could see the steps. Usually, he would descend in darkness. Tonight, he carried the book with him, his mind occupied...

Chapter Ten

When he called the second man God, David rushed out of the kitchen, through the dining room and up the stairs. He went to the computer and brought up the story the first man had been working on. He did not read what the man had written, moving through the pages until he found the blank pages he had created and the first typing he had done. He did not feel nameless as he stared at the white page, but he felt empty. He tried to tell himself how easy it had always been, having a story to tell. His work was what he called writing. He tried to capture the excitement he had when he wrote the story about his father and Juma the guide when they tracked the old elephant. When he wrote that story he was certain he had written his most self-reflexive novel, considering in it time and time again his own philosophy of composition. His work had always been his prophylactic against...

I don't know what I'm telling myself he thought.

He wanted to start in again on a new and difficult story and work attacking this thing with God that he was facing. *The concomitant fear of God,* he told himself, *has been robbing me of my ability to write until I have now begun to question whether I will ever again feel the warmth that*

came each time I understood why it was
necessary for me to write.

He could not think clearly. He was encouraged by the fact that he had correctly remembered what he had written about sex and thrilled that he had recalled how easy it had been to write the elephant scenes. Yet, he could not write. He felt for some reason as though God had taken away the entire wilderness he once played in...

Chapter Eleven

"David!" the second man called up, his voice booming.

"What do you want?" David asked.

"Come down here!"

"That sounds like an order to me," David said.

"Get the hell down here!"

David left the computer, having written nothing. He walked slowly to the landing and looked through the wall of glass. A squirrel darted diagonally along a limb in the maple, jumped without stopping from the limb to another limb in the adjacent cedar. He looked down. God was watching the squirrel, too. When the squirrel scampered down a nearby redbud and ran toward the cliff where it disappeared, God turned, a smile on his face, and looked up at David. He motioned with his right hand, inviting David to join him. Suddenly God did not seem so imposing. In fact, the smile made him appear almost human.

"I'm not God," the grizzled man said when David entered the living room. "So help me I'm not."

"I think you are," David objected.

"At least you didn't say I believe," the man laughed. "I've had a hard time trying to figure out why you suddenly appeared on that boulder by my favorite trout stream in the Black Hills, one of many stolen from the Sioux and Cheyenne..."

"I wrote about fishing in New York and in the Black Hills," David interrupted for the thought came to him and he was proud of himself. "I used that same phrase about the Indians..."

"No you didn't," the man stated. "I think you might want to read this book before we talk again.

David took the paperback from the man's right hand.

"And you might need to read the first two chapters of this," the man said.

David took the Bible and went upstairs to read.

"When you get ready to talk," the second man called, "I'll be in the bedroom behind me. I like it better than the closet. It has a floor model radio in it, an antique like me. The **Grunow** receiver picks up great but the speakers don't. I have to put my ear against it to hear."

David did not comment.

Chapter Twelve

David began to read as soon as he got upstairs. He sat on the chair at the computer, his left leg across his right with the bend of his top leg over the knee of his lower. He put the Bible on the floor to his left then he opened the novel and began to read. He liked the description of Grau du Roi, a city he knew well for he spent part of his honeymoon there.

Honeymoon? he asked himself again...

He tried to see the hotel, the canal, the fishing boats and tried harder to smell the food, especially breakfast at the café. When he read how and what the girl spoke, he could not relate to the words or to his bride who had said the same words to him. She had been wondering what he was thinking when he was not thinking.

When the girl in the novel told the man what type of woman she was, David began to get uneasy. He felt like someone had stolen parts of his life and put them on the page.

They did he said to himself as he read the page about what the townspeople wore— what he and Catherine, his wife, had worn too when they went to the Mediterranean that summer. Reading the book gave him his past, but it raised so many questions.

When he got to page seven, the author made the mistake of using his name. It was on the page as big as life: David Bourne. He read the pages about the fish the young man caught, his fish, but he got a thrill out of reading the scene. Then the author was brazen enough to write about Catherine's first boy haircut. By the end of the first chapter, anyone who read the book knew why she cut her hair—why she called herself Peter and him her girl, Catherine.

He threw the book against the exposed beam and it fell on the register, open like the book the man, Tomas, had placed on the bed.

The Garden of Eden he said to himself. *Why would anyone write about us, about our honeymoon and give the book such an absurd title?*

He picked up the Bible and read the first three chapters, not being content with reading the first two chapters as God had directed.

I've never read that before he thought. *The Garden of Eden tells how God created Adam and Eve. He commanded them not to eat from the Tree of Knowledge of Good and Evil. Why didn't I know that? Why didn't I know that a serpent tempted the man and the woman?*

David felt as though something had swept the past out of his mind. He felt as though he had never seen the sun sink golden into the azure Mediterranean. He felt like he had never been a writer. He had, he knew, worked hard at writing. Something sinister must have happened to make him forget what value he had put on personal expression and upon the integrity of writing itself.

But what? He asked himself.

Chapter Thirteen

Tomas saw her car, the woman he had promised to give a copy of his new novel. The car could have belonged to anyone in two or three counties except for the simple fact that he knew it to be hers. She was walking from Lake Cumberland Country Store toward the car as he drove past. He waved, but he did not know if she saw him. He asked her once if she could have any car that she wanted to tell him what make, model and color would be her preference.

"I used to think that if I could have any car in the world that it would be a Ferrari, but I've changed my mind," she said. "Honestly, it is just hard to beat a Corvette. So, I would have a brand new Corvette Convertible, red in color with tan interior and a tan top like this one. The new ones have 400 hp and a push button start. Very cool, I think."

He knew he could not turn around and get to the store before she drove away. If she turned right when she left the store, she could drive a couple of miles then turn left toward Columbia on 55 or keep to 127 and go toward Jamestown. He kept driving toward Wolf Creek Dam, knowing he would have to catch her some other time.

He drove past Pioneer Antiques on the left, glancing to see if the rusty 1953 Ford pick-up truck with a bullet hole in the metal above the windshield was still parked near the store, facing the road. It was. Roger, the owner of the store had told him the story behind the truck and the bullet hole. Although Tomas knew the story—had known the man who owned the truck and the man who killed him on the square in Albany—he had not realized where the truck ended up until he stopped the first time months earlier. He thought about turning in, stopping to buy a first edition of Mark Twain's *The Adventures of Tom Sawyer* and to ask Clara, a retired teacher and co-owner of the shop, to make him a pineapple milkshake. He did not stop. He glanced into his rear view mirror to see whether the woman's car was behind him.

When he had crossed Wolf Creek Dam, slowing to make the sharp left turn, he glanced into the mirror again. The car was behind now, almost a mile away on the straight stretch created by the dam, a welcome sight to any driver after so many curves behind and the many more to come ahead. He knew she would speed up crossing the dam, but she would not come up behind him for a few more miles.

In the last curve before Ryan's Grocery and the long, straight stretch of Highway 127 where Perry Neathery was killed, hit head on by a drag racer in his lane, he let off the gas, forced to slow by the two cars ahead. He followed them; she followed the three of them.

He pushed down on the button that controlled the window before he gave his signal to turn into his drive. He reached behind the driver's seat and took a book, his novel, from the box on the rear seat. He held it out the window as he waited for two cars to pass, traveling north in the lane opposite his Kia. He saw her signal flashing. He drove up even with the walk leading toward the house, and stopped, getting out.

"I didn't know whether you would follow me," Tomas said as he approached her sports car.

The woman got out, standing tall in her heels.

"I didn't know whether to or not..." she began.

"I understand," he said. "People gossip when they see a man talking to a woman..."

"They gossip when they don't see you talking to one, too," she said.

"That would be worse...I've been working out," he said, explaining his dress, sweats, a t-shirt and running shoes.

"I can see that," she said. "Do you work out in Russell County?"

"No," he answered. "I work out at the college."

"What is it you do there, exactly?" she asked.

"I'm the director of one of the federal programs," he said, and asked: "are you still working?"

'Yes," she said. "If I had known when I got out of school I would end up doing what I am, I would have looked harder for something better—something I'd rather be doing."

"Hindsight," he said. "If we could have that same understanding before we chose careers, love, or divorce, wouldn't it have been great. I don't think anyone will see you here."

"I always wondered what it looked like back here. I like this."

"I do, too," he said, walking to his vehicle.

He opened the rear door and held up a book of poetry.

"Do you have this book?" he asked.

"No," she said.

He dug in the box and found a second book of poetry that he knew was in it.

"What about this one?"

"I don't have it either," she said.

He shut both doors and looked at the woman.

"What's happening with the ghost?" she asked.

"She's still active. My sister sees her every day and most nights. She heard her one night this week, walking through the house. Then she heard a loud noise like a bar or some other piece of furniture being turned over. The next night my brother-in-law heard the same thing and the third night my sister heard it again. They never found anything out of place when they looked. You should have visited them on Halloween," he said.

"I don't think so," she said.

"I've seen the ghost in my house," he said.

"Get out of here!"

"He was standing by the fireplace. Actually, it was a blue mist I saw, formless except for the head that had disheveled hair, all its facial features and a beard. I could have imagined it, but it looked real to me when I woke up on the sofa. My heart beat fast," he said.

"I couldn't handle that," she said.

"I've got something else to give you if you have time," he said, crossing the driveway and the concrete patio.

"Sure," she said, following.

He had trouble getting the key in the lock. He said something about it, but the words were forgotten as quickly as they left his mouth. As he entered the kitchen, he closed the doors to the utility. He heard her chuckle behind him. He went to the counter and picked up a business card and gave it to her.

"I found you an illustrator," he said. "She will do your books at no charge."

"Why would she do that?" she asked.

"She likes illustrating children's books," he said.

"Have you seen any of her work?"

"I saw the books she had with her last Saturday at the Western Kentucky Book Expo. They were nice," he assured her. "She also paints gold bricks."

"I don't know what that means," she said.

"In the early days of the Gold Rush, con artists would gold plate bricks and pass them off as solid gold bars."

"I see," she said, turning to leave.

"Just send me her email address," he said, following her. "I want to get her to do a book my son wrote. It's about a duck. I told her about it. She wants to do it, too."

"I'll get it to you," she said, walking across the patio toward her car. "I like the house."

"I should have shown you the rest of it," he said. "If you've got a minute..."

"Sure," she said, putting the three books through the open window and on the driver's seat.

She followed him into the house the second time and into the living room. Tomas pointed at the spinning wheel.

"That belonged to a Kentucky governor," he said.

"Really?"

"One born in Clinton County when it was part of Wayne County..."

He walked to the fireplace and opened the glass door near the wall.

"He was standing like this," Tomas said, referring to the ectoplasm, the anomaly again.

The woman shook her head. She did not voice concern this time, following him toward the bedroom. He switched on the overhead light.

"That also belonged to the same governor," he said, pointing toward a love seat across the room.

"I didn't know you liked antiques," she said.

"I do," he said.

"Dad does, too," she added.

"You may go upstairs if you like, but be careful with the steps."

He followed her upstairs. She turned left away from the loft bedroom and stepped toward the banister.

"I love this view," she said, looking through the pyramid of glass. "I've never been in an A-frame before. I never would have imagined one could look like this. The view is beautiful. I just love it."

"I like it here," he said, backing into the loft bedroom and flipping the light switch. "It's private. I'm getting things fixed up."

"Do you always keep it like this?" she asked when she entered the bedroom.

"Yes," he said, pleased that she had noticed. "I take that as a compliment. The closet, where I told you the first writer was, is here off the bathroom."

She followed him in and out as he told her how he sometimes felt as though a second ghost lived in the closet in the bedroom. He told her he had not seen it and talked about what he had already written.

"Would you like to read it?" he asked.

"Sure," she said.

He turned on the computer and got up to give her the chair when the file opened. He kneeled, reading as she read, wondering whether his words were of any interest to her.

"This is intense," she commented, "but easier to read than the other."

"That's what I hoped for," he said. "I'm trying to write like he did, short chapters."

"I never realized how much detail has to go into a novel. It seems to me a reader will have to know a lot about his book to understand yours."

"Probably," he said, thinking: *I'll have to come back, fill in any holes so the story stands alone.*

When she finished reading, she stood up, looking up and through the skylight.

"Put a new roof on and a new skylight," he said. "I've got to fix the ceiling where the old skylight leaked."

She did not say anything. He wondered what she was thinking. He knew without being able to read her thoughts that he would never know, but he was also thinking. What he could not understand was why Aristotle's words came to mind, those calling woman an incomplete or mutilated man. He felt like the woman would disagree with Aristotle. Perhaps she would call him a man who was afraid of a woman's sexuality, of her intelligence, and most of all of her emotions.

I'll loan you my copy as soon as I finish taking notes," he told her, remembering the book.

"I'll check one out of the library," she said.

He did not tell her the book might be hard to find. He turned off the computer and followed her to the landing, knowing that he would search the Internet from his office and order a book.

"I see what you mean," she said as she started down the steps, stopping as she spoke.

"Just be careful," he cautioned.

She turned left at the bottom of the stairs and went toward the kitchen door.

"I didn't know if I could tempt you with the book or not," Tomas said as she opened the door.

She chuckled.

"If you don't like the books," he said, "just bring them back."

"I like reading your books," she said without looking back. He closed the door; she turned left, crossing the patio, moving quickly toward her car. As she opened the door, she looked around.

"My brother wouldn't want me to tell this," she said, "but you know the house we grew up in?"

"Sure," he answered.

"We were downstairs when we first moved in. He wouldn't say it was true if you asked him, but we heard high heels on the hardwood floors upstairs. We thought somebody was in the house. My brother said he wished he had a gun so we could go up there. I called him a chicken because I knew what would happen. We went upstairs. There was no one in the house but the two of us. There's no one living there now. I think it was a ghost. I read a few things about haunted houses after that. One article suggested that sometimes something belonging to the ghost is the reason for any haunting. I remembered an old Victrola my brother bought at a flea market. It wouldn't work so he left it on the back porch. When I talked him into giving it away, we never heard footsteps again. "

"Maybe we all live in a world of dreams, of shadows moving about, he thought.

"I really love your house," she said.

"Thank you...you have to come back and read more as I write this one," he said. "I'm having fun with it. Better yet, come back and write your own."

Chapter Fourteen

Tomas stood in the driveway, lonely but proud to be alive. His minister, Harlan Ogle might not approve of a man feeling pride, but judging the man by his own literary pursuits, which Tomas did, he thought *the preacher has had this feeling, too.*

He walked to the deck from the concrete patio, the deck that covered half of the gazebo, front and right side. The other half was built, one-quarter on treated timbers high enough above the cliff to be level with the deck on the other two sides while the last one-quarter of the other half had been built on a gentle slope.

He stood in the sun on a bright, unseasonably hot early fall afternoon that he was glad he had experienced. He could not have asked for a more perfect day, a breeze moving maple, poplar, locust and other leaves from west to east across the rolling lawn. If the wind intensified as the DJ in Cookeville predicted, he would not have to rake many leaves for they would end up at the bottom of the cliff and form new soil slowly.

He wanted to go inside and write but he decided to take off his shirt and feel the sun on his skin.

In rare moments like this, time matters he thought. *Life matters, even a life without love.*

Writing for him was becoming easier; almost second nature and he did not feel complete if, on any given day, he did not write. He could find pleasure in thought or in action. In words, he could advance his consciousness; feel spontaneous and integrated into the larger scheme of things. He called those things pure awareness, a fleeting state of being.

He knew, in spite of his enjoyment of the fleeting moments, that he wanted to write more than he wanted to tan. He realized, however, that life is more than what simply happens between the pages of a book. He also understood that good writing makes the reader see, feel, hear and enjoy. Human imagination has no limits...

Tomas put his shirt on and went inside.

Chapter Fifteen

David picked up the novel and began to read it in spite of his anger toward the author. He read because he wanted to understand how the author knew so much about him, things he had forgotten or never known. He began to discover something about the writer. The man could create characters so complex by having them say next to nothing. The dialogue did not carry the story. It was most often laconic and breezy, but what disturbed him most was the fact that the words were precisely hers and his.

He appreciated the easy, free flow of the narrative, thinking the man must have written it in a few weeks. What he could not understand was what statement he intended to make. He felt the same old restlessness and impatience with the normal course of the world that he felt the time Catherine invited Marita to travel with them. As he reread the scene, he understood that he needed to cross the threshold from the now to those moments with them. He hoped he could do that and that in the process he would see what had happened to him—them. There was life in reading the book.

He wished he could write again. He wished he could remember what his first novel was like. He'd like to be reading it. He remembered reading the reviews, hundreds of them. He remembered it was successful, but he sat confused, with no feeling for what he had written. It was a story that no longer meant anything. He hated that thought and asked: *How could the words have just disappeared from my memory?* He turned back to the novel in his hands, hating the writer for knowing that he had lied to Catherine.

When reading and thinking no longer did any good, he let his anger reside and took a pencil from a wooden bowl behind Tomas' desk and a black notebook from a folder to the right of the bowl, one with no writing in it, and tried to step outside himself, tried to write.

When he put the notebook inside the folder later, there were still no words in it.

Chapter Sixteen

The moment David put the notebook away God appeared in the loft bedroom.

"You ready to talk yet?" God asked.

"I'm too mad to talk," he said.

"Read it!" God ordered. "And when you know that I'm not God, we'll talk."

"I'm going to read something else," David said, getting up and going to the bed.

"Read the god-damned book!" God cursed as David picked up the book Tomas had placed open above the stacks of articles.

"I'm curious why he put this book there," David said, reading.

When he scanned the two pages, he handed the book to God. God hesitated then read quickly. David picked up the pencil from the desk again and bent to get the notebook.

"Write the words that are the most important ones that you read," David directed, extending the notebook in his right hand.

God looked angry as he took the pencil and notebook, writing words quickly though.

"You wrote: **she said, 'men are frantic to know what is certain to give them pain**,'" David said. "You are God! As you wrote those words, they appeared on the backs of my eyelids..."

God stomped from the loft, jarring the stairs as he descended.

Who am I? Where did I come from? David asked himself.

David walked to the loft. Looking down, he yelled: "what are you trying to do to me!"

"Read the fucking book, you mindless fart! Placate me!" God fumed.

Chapter Seventeen

The moment God called up to David, David already knew he was going to tell him he was writing.

"I'm writing!"

I wish you wouldn't shout David thought, crouching forward, shrugging his shoulders as he did for he sensed that God might hear him and punish him.

"I know," David said. "You have written Garden of Eden; you've written Eden from Hebrew *Gan Eden.*"

"Up yours!"

"You'll regret saying that, later," David raised his voice, careful not to shout too much.

"What!"

"I said that to a waiter once when he told me his establishment was not a beer place. I still regret it…"

"You fucker, you didn't say that!"

"Did too!"

"I'm writing!" God shouted.

"Garden of Eden is the location of the story told in *Genesis* two and three," David read the words as they appeared on his eyelids for he had bowed his head and closed his eyes.

"Part of the creation belief of the Abrahamic religions!" God shouted.

"I read it," David said.

"Tell me what you remember," God called up.

"God created Adam and Eve then commanded them not to eat from the Tree of Knowledge of Good and Evil. A serpent tempted the woman; she tempted the man. They ate the fruit. God expelled them and stationed cherubim and a flaming sword at the entrance to the garden in order to keep man from returning and eating from the Tree of Life."

"Well hell! You're not mindless after all! Christians think the snake was the Devil, though there's no mention of that in the Book."

What's the Devil? David thought, but he did not ask for he did not want God to call him mindless again. In the book, Devil was what he had called Catherine.

"The Devil exists in many religions. He's the major personified spirit of evil, ruler of Hell, and foe of God," God said.

David was certain God could read his thoughts!

Am I the Devil now? David asked himself.

"Women used to call me a handsome devil," God said.

David was confused by those words.

"Finish the god-damned book," God said, the anger gone from his voice.

It must not be a sin for God to take his own name in vain, David thought.

Chapter Eighteen

When David read the paragraph about Marita reading the stories at the bar after he had finished writing them, he became disoriented again. He could not remember that happening to them. He could not recall that he thought it ill mannered to want to read over her shoulder while she read—to want to see her expressions.

What he could remember clearly was Tomas sitting in the floor by the woman whose name he did not know—Tomas looking up, eyes darting from the white page on the glass to the woman's face. From beneath the bed, he remembered watching them, fascinated.

In the book the way the writer wrote of him watching Marita read the stories about Africa disturbed him. He realized, however, that the book was fiction, and the author was only using the technique that worked best for him as he created the scene.

Detail is supposed to stimulate memory he thought. *The details don't do it for me. This book is fiction based upon my life. It is nothing more.*

As he read, he could not recapture other scenes from his past that changed his thinking. He had seen Tomas sit on the floor, inches from where he lay. He had seen the woman's face as she read. If the scenes were real, he should be able to close his eyes and see Catherine's face or Marita's. He could not and neither could he see an elephant with tusks so long that a man could not reach the top of them as they leaned against a wall. He could not see what kind of wall it was. He could not tell himself anything about his childhood. He could not remember being sick, the smell of bread baking, the sound of drums in the village, or the house he grew up in. The biggest shock, however, was his inability to see his mother's face or Kibo, his faithful dog, his friend for...

"How long?" he asked.

He had no idea. It was as though he was not of a people—as though no schools, churches, clubs of any kind had been part of his life. And the women, the lesbians, Catherine and Marita, he wanted to remember them for he had made love to both, never both at once, or so it was written. What he needed to do was believe that he loved them and they loved each other if that is what lesbians do.

He had to keep reading. He was nearing the end. He was about to begin **Book Four**. He looked at the number of pages in the novel. There were two hundred forty-seven pages, meaning, as he calculated, he only had thirty-eight more to read.

After thirty-eight more pages he would know everything. He would know what happened to Catherine, to Marita and to David

Bourne. He needed to know whether his African stories were as successful as his first novel.

He caught a glimpse of God sticking his head around the doorway and just as quickly the doorway was empty. He smiled. God had caught him reading, but God should have known he was reading without having to look. He did not know whether someone had taught him that God is all-knowing or whether he had learned it by himself, knowledge gained thus, he reasoned, makes its way into a person's imagination.

He could remember the first day he saw God. He was sitting on a boulder, a large rock wet with dew, and God was wading in the stream, fly-fishing, masterful, holding an unseen rod, letting out line, retrieving it and going through the motions of catching one trout after the other only to release each of them.

I bet Catherine killed me David thought, flipping back to the beginning of the book to reread the page where she said she would destroy him.

That's what she did he said *and that's the day I landed on that rock...*

He wanted to skip to the end of the book, but he heard Tomas climbing the stairs. The man's footsteps were heavier than God's unless God was angry, descending.

Chapter Nineteen

As Tomas climbed the stairs, he thought about the email he had sent to the woman whose choice in cars was a red Corvette. He wrote: ***just some food for thought and a request that you start writing something soon, a poem, the children's book, or some journal entries. You might have to think of me as your ghost, not a threatening one, but one pushing you in the direction that you want to go already***.

Tomas noticed the book as soon as he turned on the light in the loft bedroom. It was closed and lying across the bed. He had not left it that way. He picked it up, opened it, and it opened at the page he had been reading, page ninety-three. He read again Marguerite's telling Armand how men are frantic to know what is certain to give them pain.

He closed the book and went to his computer. He put the book between his knees so he could turn on the pc and monitor. While he waited for the desktop to load, he looked down at the book. He saw two pages turned down in the book that had fallen open, creating three sections, of which the first was larger than the second but smaller than the third.

I never turn down pages he said to himself.

"Underlined!" Tomas exclaimed when he glanced at page sixty-eight, the first dog-eared page.

It may sound childish to tell you all these details he read the underlined words.

"In ink, damn it!" he looked over his right shoulder. The landing as far as the banister was all he could see. Beyond, there was darkness.

He opened the book to the next page.

She looked ravishing he read. The words were also underlined in ink.

Tomas leaned back in his chair, his hands cupping his head. He could not write. He tried, instead, to convince himself that he had overlooked the dog-eared pages and the underlined sentences.

"Two years at least," he said aloud, remembering how long it had been since he had read the novel.

He turned off the computer and the monitor and looked over his left shoulder. He pushed back the chair with difficulty for the wheels had sunk into the carpet as they always did. He put the book on the foot of the bed and stood up; taking one step with his right leg toward the bed; turning on his heel; bringing his left leg in one motion behind the chair. He reached over the chair with his right arm, tilted the chair backward by the seat with his left, and shoved the chair under the desk. With his feet, he worked the depressions out of the carpet.

He picked up *Camille* without opening it and took the book to the landing where he placed it on the top shelf of the bookcase. He reached around the bedroom door and turned out the light. He took his time going down the stairs in darkness. He went to the downstairs bedroom and, without turning on the light, made his way to the closet. He took out a comforter, a quilt, and a pillow. In the living room, he made his bed for the night. There was enough light from the security light near the garage to cast shadows on the wall. He closed his eyes. When he did, he saw a stream flowing toward him. The water gave off light, bright and white like it was reflecting moonlight. Dark ripples moved over the stream...

He opened his eyes.

Was that a shadow? He asked himself, convinced he had seen something—some movement from the fireplace into the dining room hall.

He closed his eyes again, but he could not see the stream. He knew that, in neglecting the dream that it, like a person, had given up, choosing not to return.

Chapter Twenty

"Come walk with me," God said when David came downstairs the next morning.

"I want to read while he is gone..."

"I've read his novels and his books of poetry. He knows the only way to forget his personal grief is to write. Reminds me of what I told F. Scott once. Told him to use his hurt... Told him all he was is a writer. Couldn't convince him to forget he loved that woman though even when everybody told him she was jealous of his work. The source of this man's work is his own life. What his eyes see and his heart feels get poured onto the page. He lives in his words. He has seen much more of the world than most of his neighbors. He listens more than he talks. He thinks quickly and is not afraid."

"I think you read his heart—not his words. He got mad at you..."

"When he read *Camille*, you mean?"

"He likes books."

"He knows I'm here. He's seen me. I just wanted to tell him I know he knows. I'm curious about something and I let him know the object of my curiosity. The object is his pain and he thinks it is his being; it is not his joy as he feels it should be. It is only his becoming. He's got to learn to recognize the difference."

"Centering a story about a woman has to be challenging," David said, guessing woman to be God's object.

"A woman is always a challenge," God said. "Who can know how she feels in her own skin?"

"You should know," David said.

"Because I'm God, you mean?"

"If you weren't God—were just a writer, how would you write about a woman?"

"I'd write about her being on her back on a bed," God laughed. "It would never do to try to get inside her head."

"What would your critics say?"

"Critics be damned! I'll write for you if you walk with me..."

"What will you write?" David asked.

"What would you have me write?"

"Write it the way it was."

"I can do that," God said, "but what if I write it the way you think it was so you can know that I am not God."

"Open your sails," David said, hurrying into the kitchen and out the door where he stood on the patio, waiting.

The oaks off the patio still held most of their leaves, but the ground was littered with maple, poplar, sycamore and redbud leaves. David waited for God to come out and join him. When he did not, he stepped from the patio and followed the walk to the deck.

"What kept you?" God called from the front deck where he sat on a rail, moving his legs to the rhythm of a music David could not hear.

"You did," David said.

"I came out the front. It was you who kept me..."

"So write," David said.

"What was ever real for you?"

"Africa!"

"Do you know some African parents cut off their daughters clits to keep them from feeling pleasure in it like a man does? Is that what you would have me write?"

"No," David said, for he understood nothing that God had said.

"Do you remember the spur fouls?"

"Of course I do," David said. "I killed two..."

"Here!" God called tossing a slingshot he had taken from the closet in the bedroom where the antique radio was. "Grab some of those round creek gravel down here by the steps and kill me a squirrel or two in this maple."

David stirred the stones with his finger and chose three of the bigger round stones.

"Eight limbs up and toward the redbud," God said.

"I see it," David said, taking aim.

"Not even close," God taunted after the stone went wide and to the right.

The second stone came out of the slingshot and veered left, striking the cedar that had forced the redbud to lean out from its shade to find enough sunshine to sustain it.

While David took aim with a third stone in the pouch he squeezed tightly, God fired a pistol, a 32-20 Smith & Wesson he had found in the downstairs bedroom where he spent most of his time listening to AM or Short-wave broadcasts. He had loaded it with Remington high velocity center fire lead tip cartridges designed for use on small and medium game at close range.

"Now that's a sweet shooting gun," God said, stroking the warm barrel. "Remember how warm a woman feels?"

David tried to remember, but he did not answer.

"Fetch!" God said, pointing toward the squirrel. "I'll put more wood on the fire. I'll cook it for you in the fireplace. You skin it. I'll cook it."

"Skin it!"

"Hell yes! Take this *CASE-XX* knife I found in a kitchen drawer; cut around the hind legs and make a slit from one leg to the other; cut the tail off; pull its britches down; put a foot on each of its pant legs; and give a quick upward jerk. Cut its head off because I hit it between the eyes then gut it and bring it to me."

"I thought you were going to write," David taunted.

"This is how it is," God whispered into David's ear. "After I feed you, I'm going to write you into Africa so you can see if that's how it was."

Chapter Twenty-one

"How was it?" God asked.

"It was good," David said, lying, for he had no memory of ever having eaten food even though he had read in the novel that he ate daily.

"Squirrel looks like a rat when it's cooking on a skewer, but you can't think about that when you eat it," God laughed, picking his teeth with the knife David used to dress the rodent. He smiled, thinking how the word dress did not seem to be the appropriate choice to describe the process of skinning an animal.

David looked into God's eyes and looked away when contact was made. He had hoped to discover whether God's eyes were alive or not. When he had read the scene where his father killed the bull elephant, he felt a chill for the author had described the elephant looking at him and him understanding that the elephant's eye was the most alive thing he, a disheartened boy, had ever seen. What troubled him now was the fact that he had no idea what life should look like in another's eyes. What also troubled him was the food. He never knew God ever ate.

"Should have coined the phrase with undress," God said, climbing from the rail above the deck.

"What are you talking about?" David asked.

"Skinning," God said. "Field dressing game... Seems to me it's more a taking off than a putting on... Wouldn't you agree?"

"It would seem so," David said.

"Did you know a man is only a spirit clothed in skin?"

"I didn't know that," David answered.

"Do you remember the last woman you undressed?"

"Yes," David lied without hesitation.

"Of course you don't," God laughed. "I'm ready to write now. Fetch me a pencil and paper."

"Come inside with me now. Come upstairs and write on the ViewSonic," David said, opening the sliding glass door that led into the living room. When he entered the room, he smelled strange odors. To his surprise, God followed.

David hurried up the steps to turn on the computer and monitor. He motioned for God to come to the chair and sit until the desktop appeared. God obliged, slumping forward with his elbows on his legs.

Do you know what this place needs?"
God asked.

"No... Yes... Maybe," David answered.

"Well, I know," God said. "It needs a cat.
Needs one that is polydactyl like the one my
friend, a ship's captain, gave me when I lived in
Cuba... It's too bad I never brought those cats to
Florida or Idaho. Course you don't know what
polydactyl means, do you? It means the cat has
extra toes, mostly on front paws, but now and
again one is born with six toes on its back feet."

"I figured you were going to say it's not
good for the man to be alone," David said.

God chuckled.

David smiled.

"Life is full of duality," God said. "One
moment is dramatic, inspirational and the next
mundane, every day moments. The two women
who came here are opposites. Either one remind
you of anyone?"

David wanted to say yes, but he could
not.

God began to type and the words
appeared on the screen and on David's eyelids,
for he had closed them to see if he was still in
tune with God's writing. He was, reading: **In**

Africa, the Masai know that when God came to work his will with the world, he found a hunting tribe, an elephant, and a serpent.

"Do you know that most African cultures did not fear God as you do? You close your eyes and say you see the words I write. I'm having a hard time with that. I'd rather you treat me like Kintu, the first man to come down from heaven to Africa, than fear me. He was isolated and unknown even to the other folks in heaven until other sons of heaven came down and their sister. Kintu married her. I'm not God, but somehow I'm your creator in this nightmare of a story. You should not revere me. Knowing that, do you want me to write you back to Africa?" God asked.

"Please," David said.

God looked at David and began to type without watching the screen. David closed his eyes, reading the words as they appeared: **When David was young, six or seven years old at least but no older, he went outside the village with an African boy of ten. The older boy ran to the fruit trees where a group of monkeys were feasting. Since it, beginning that very morning, was to be his job to protect the fruit, he began to throw stones at the hungry monkeys. David began to throw stones and sticks at the monkeys, too. The monkeys did not leave the trees. The boys missed the monkeys with every stone, every stick they threw. The monkeys caught every stick and**

stone that was thrown at them. Then they began to throw them back at the boys. The monkeys never missed. When the boys ran back into the village, how those monkeys laughed.

"Welcome back," God laughed at David. "And how was Africa?"

'I'm going to finish the book now," David said, thinking: *I wish I could tell God how I not only see his words—how I become a participant in his work. I am his creation, but I am alive in his stories—more alive than I am in the novel I'm reading.*

David did not tell God what he had thought, for he understood that God already knew all things.

"Ain't it strange how you do everything I write," God said and David became convinced that God was all-powerful.

Chapter Twenty-two

It had been a long day for Tomas, one that began with forty minutes of driving to work at Lindsey Wilson College. He worked at the computer until Director Staff Meeting.

What Dean Adams, Vice-President for Student Services and Enrollment Management, said during his wrap-up of the meeting struck home for Tomas.

"Be aware of what's going on around campus as the semester winds down," Dean had said. "Let's all remember never to leave our first love, the students, as we go about our business. Also, think about how you would answer the question: what empirical evidence is there to show that what we do adds value to education?"

After lunch, Tomas went back to his computer. The Annual Performance Report he worked on was due at the end of the month. He had input data until eleven o'clock then read his messages and emailed his secretary before leaving for Hindman where he would speak to a Writers' Group about Kentucky authors.

The woman had sent him an email in answer to his last two messages. She had written *I don't mind your emails; I have very few friends so I enjoy having someone to talk to with common interests. I look forward to reading more of your book.*

When he got to Hazard, he saw first hand the results of mountaintop removal, a process coal companies were utilizing to remove the black veins of coal. Although he had heard about mountaintop removal and seen a couple of news report on the practice, he did not comprehend the scope of what was happening in east Kentucky. He pulled to the shoulder of the road and watched a dump truck deposit coal into a tipple. Beneath the tipple, boxcars rounded high with black coal stretched beyond his view.

When he started driving again, he looked to his right. Where a hardwood forest and a towering ridge stood when he last drove through Hazard the forest was gone. In its place, a lone backhoe worked it way around the mountain, dumping earth and stone into what once was a valley. He looked for water below, but did not see a stream.

A group of writers with ties to the region, thirty-five inspired by their tour of eastern Kentucky had written a book, *Missing Mountains: We went to the mountaintop but it wasn't there.* He had ordered the book from Amazon earlier that morning. He knew most of the writers from reading their works for the contributors list included Silas House, Bobbie

Ann Mason, Mary Ann Taylor-Hall, Gurney Norman, Steven Cope, Bob Sloan, Gwyn Hyman Rubio, George Ella Lyon, Loyal Jones, Ed McClanahan, Chris Holbrook, Anne Shelby and Wendell Berry, a poet, novelist and essayist critics admired for his agrarian and social philosophies. He knew the volume would speak out against the mining practice, new to the east Kentucky mountains. He had worked with Loyal Jones, Gurney Norman and George Ella Lyon when he and Jim Wayne Miller designed a Kentucky Literature training program for English teachers in grades five through twelve for the local school district. He hoped their words would not fall on deaf ears.

Mountaintop removal for coal mining took on a new meaning for him when he watched the backhoe bite into the hillside again and again. The coal companies in eastern Kentucky, as well as the companies in other coal producing states, once employed hundreds of workers to mine into a mountain and remove the coal. Ten workers to go up to a mountain, blast the top off of it, extract the coal, and dump the former mountaintop into the valleys below— such a small group was the total work force at sites such as the one he viewed on the side of the road at dusk. He imagined that with the price of oil being high coal was following suit, going up as well and creating a boom time. He asked himself how many residents of Hazard did not love green mountains in spring, red, gold and yellow landscapes in autumn like the one before him had been for eons. He wondered how many locals placed little or no value on mountains if they could be mined.

While he watched, he remembered going to Ohio for the first time. There were at least five of them in a 1957 Chevrolet station wagon, his father and mother, and his sister and brother. He was the fifth. Maybe there was a sixth, another sister. Depending on the exact year, which he did not remember, maybe there had been seven of them or eight at the most, also sisters. He knew the three younger girls had not been born so there were not eleven, his parents, seven girls and two boys, in the car. What he remembered most about the family reunion was the coalmine they went to near the creek behind the house where his Aunt and Uncle, their two children, Jimmy and Debbie, and a dog lived. The mine was boarded up, but they looked through broken planks into the dark man-made cave.

After a few years, three to five, his family went back for a funeral. His mother got angry as they crossed the rolling hills from Columbus to Steubenville. She was not angry with any of them, but with the coal companies that had stripped the land in the intervening years. To him, the land looked wounded. Deep, open trenches scarred the landscape. It was a time when coal companies were not required to reclaim the earth or if laws to force such reclamations existed, no one enforced them.

He remembered swimming in Island Creek with his cousins, Betsey, Kay, and Bill. The creek, in those days was clear and cold.

He heard the adults talk about mining that night. His uncle had told them there was a consensus among the adults in his community that coal had regenerated a much needed boom only to be followed by a bust. On Coal Hill that night a man played music with his Uncle Walter, singing about the mines that had played out in their lifetime.

"Poverty ain't no friend to the land," he sang. "The streams run black with silt and sand, but coal puts money in this miner's hand."

When he was grown, he and his father returned to the region to hunt with one of his mother's brothers, Red. On the steepest mountain outside Richmond where his uncle lived, a dragline, the largest in the world removed coal day and night. The noise of that operation was continuous. He thought about the man who sang his ditty those many years before, but did not ask his uncle if the man was still alive.

"Stripping coal's necessary," a woman who owned a restaurant on the road toward Richmond told his father when they stopped to eat breakfast that first morning before he drove the final three or four miles to his brother-in-law's home.

"We're farmers," Tomas' father said. "The land gives us hope."

"We depend on steel mills and mills need coal. My son used to fight the coal companies when he was first out of college. He gave up— bailed out. He sells insurance in New Jersey these days and travels a lot. Coal doesn't bring jobs like mining once did. Someone to run the technology and truck drivers are all a company needs these days. Sometimes I feel sorry for the land myself, but then I think about this business I have here. It ain't much, but it's mine. Just wait until you see the lights on that mountain tonight," she told them. "Looks like a city up there..."

When they hunted that night, they did see the lights. His uncle took them to land the coal company owned.

"Why is this so level?" his father asked.

"Coal company stripped the top off to get the vein of coal and fixed it like this... They say it will be land a farmer will want to buy, fence, and graze cattle. They say Wintersville and Richmond can build houses or businesses on each end and meet in the middle to be one large city. As for me, I don't expect to see such things in my lifetime. The coal company owns it. They can say what they want," his uncle explained.

It was almost ten o'clock at night when Tomas got home. He had talked about Kentucky authors with a group of twenty writers. He had been to Hindman once with Jim Wayne Miller, an Appalachian scholar, poet and novelist, trying to recruit an author for their Kentucky Literature teachers' training project. They had driven from Bowling Green to visit James Still, author of *River of Earth*, a story of mountain people with disappointed hopes. His characters lived in coal camps and on small farms in Appalachia. He agreed to read for the teachers.

When he walked into the kitchen from the patio, he smelled wood smoke. He went to the fireplace, opened the glass doors and stirred the ashes with the brass shovel on the hearth that he always used to empty ashes from the firebox into the ash dump in front of the grate. There were no red coals in the ashes, but he found many bones that he judged to be those of a squirrel. Before he built the first fire of the season, he found the skeleton of a bird, its bones and feathers, in the firebox. He realized that the chimney with its three red-orange liners open to the world would be the scene of similar accidents anytime a bird or small climbing animal, by design or misfortune, ended up in the firebox. As he closed the fire screen and glass door, he wondered why the bones were scattered. There was no complete skeleton like there had been of the bird.

He was too tired to write, but he went upstairs with the folder of materials he had taken with him to Hindman. He picked up the other folder in the floor and added pictures and reviews of *The Garden of Eden*. He put the folder on the foot of the bed. He took time to load eight images from a diskette into his documents, my pictures folder. The images, as a slideshow, would be his screen saver. After he had finished, he turned out the light, and went downstairs.

He was too tired to fall asleep at once. He reflected on what the woman had also written in her email: ***I am writing a little bit but it is hard for me to stay focused on one thing right now. My life is sort of scattered at this point. & nbsp; I did write the children's book; I'll send it to you along with some "poetry" when I polish it off. Please understand that my poems are in no order, they're more just my feelings recorded in short fragments. So, if I should send them to you for review, feel free to mark them up; I know that they're not in correct form***.

Tomas woke with a start. It was the ringing of a telephone that jarred him out of a deep sleep. He sat up on the sofa and picked up his cell phone, attached to its charger. It was not his cell phone that rang, he realized as he pushed the green button to answer the call. In the illuminated light, he saw that it was 4:01. He did not have a line-based telephone in the A-frame.

Chapter Twenty-three

When David finished reading the final pages of *The Garden of Eden*, he put the book on the foot of the bed and stared at the computer screen. The book ended with him knowing more about his father, having rewritten most of the African hunting story that Catherine destroyed when she burned his manuscript. It also ended with him writing, recalling every sentence, line and word he had created when he first wrote the work.

The end of the book did not help David as he looked at the blank, white Microsoft Word page. He knew nothing of such things as those recorded by the author Ernest Hemingway. He had never heard of the writer.

He started to get up and get the notebook and pencil but saw another book by Ernest Hemingway on the Office Depot box beneath the computer desk. He picked it up and began to read. Even though he had no clue as to the author's reputation, what he learned from all he read in the new book and what he had read about his own life convinced him that the man could compress scenes.

A Farewell to Arms moved, but in *The Garden of Eden* there had been many pages of clear prose that were an implicit judgment of all writing. The Hemingway voice was beginning to speak to him.

On page twenty-five, David discovered that the nurse, Miss Barkley, was also named Catherine. He closed the book with his left hand and saw God's picture on the back cover. God was Earnest Hemingway! He read thirteen lines of Ernest Hemingway's biography and read the fourteenth line aloud: ***He died in Idaho in 1961.***

Chapter Twenty-four

"You ready to talk now?" Ernest Hemingway asked David.

'What should I call you?"

"Some called me Hemingway; some called me E. H. or Hem; you can call me Papa, a suitable enough nickname since you are my creation."

"I've got to read some more," David said, calling him no name at all.

"I can tell you all you want to know about *A Farewell to Arms,*" Hemingway said.

"I was never alive, was I?"

"No, David, except those parts of you that were me."

"I need to read the pages in that folder," David said, pointing toward the bed. "They're about you. There are biographies and reviews and pictures."

"I can save you the trouble," Hemingway said. "Just ask me what you want to know."

"I don't know enough to ask," David lamented.

"When you get to the reviews," Hemingway said, "call me."

"I will," David said, remembering the scene in *The Garden of Eden* where clippings of reviews had come to him in the mail and how in the book he had felt as though they had nothing to do with him or his words.

"I'd like to hear what they say about me now…"

"Since you died?" David asked, interrupting.

"Died?" Hemingway asked and laughed loudly as he went down the steps.

Chapter Twenty-five

At 4:01, Tomas sat up quickly, moving toward the ringing telephone. Again, it was not his cell phone that woke him. By the time the phone rang for the third time, he was in the right corner of the living room with his ear within four inches of the carpet. The ringer was that of an older rotary model. He was tempted to pick up the receiver and answer: *hello.*

There is no phone he reminded himself and went back to the sofa. He did not fall asleep anytime soon.

David watched Tomas from the landing, hoping the man would not look up on one hand, but wishing he would on the other. When Tomas slept again, he went back into the loft bedroom and picked up a folder, the one that Tomas usually left unopened on the antique bed. As he read, he began to understand what the critics meant when they wrote that Hemingway was the source of his material and that the jumpstart to his work was his own life.

If that is true David asked *what do I make of me? How can I be only what his eyes saw and heart felt? I have to be more than mere words he wrote—more than his imagination could fathom. I cannot be only a man's fiction.*

"I can't read your mind," Hemingway said, interrupting David.

"I don't know whether to believe you or not. Why did you call me David?" David asked without turning to face Hemingway.

"David is a Biblical name," Hemingway said. "David was the second king of Judah and Israel. According to the Book, he slew the Philistine giant Goliath with a sling and succeeded Saul as king. He was a writer like I was—like I wrote you to be. In Hebrew, the name stands for **beloved**. He saw a woman naked and sent her husband, Uriah, to the front line knowing he would be killed. In war, David, men always die like dogs. King David had my weakness for a beautiful woman. I gave you that same weakness. You could not say no to Catherine any more than Adam could to Eve. By the way, Catherine originates from a Greek word meaning **pure.**"

"And you made fun of me by giving me the last name Bourne when I was not born at all," David said.

"Not at all," Hemingway said. "Bourne is a noun, an archaic word from French, actually Old French, and from Medieval Latin. It means **a destination** or **a goal—a boundary** or **a limit.** I liked it because in Old English it also meant **a small stream** or **a brook.**"

"Maybe that explains me appearing on that slick rock where you were fishing or dancing or whatever it was you were doing!"

"The man is awake," Hemingway whispered, scurrying out of the loft bedroom and down the steps before Tomas came out of the living room and started upstairs.

Chapter Twenty-six

After Tomas left the next morning, David began to read more about the man he had mistakenly called God. What impressed him most were the statements that were direct quotes and quotes from his work. When he read that Hemingway said he wrote as though he had a tape recorder in his head, he remembered Tomas telling the second woman that he wrote from his memory as though he were listening to a tape recorder. He closed his eyes and looked up and toward the left. He had observed Tomas routinely doing that as he wrote. To his surprise, he could see images. It was not the world he saw, but only that book about his life...

My life he lamented. *I can never create a world in my own image the way Hemingway did or Tomas does. I can't pick and choose the elements that are necessary for me to use to create a world or another person.*

David began to read again the articles that Tomas had gathered. His memory was limited to the thirty chapters of one book. The articles pained him. It was Hemingway who liked to think about safaris to Africa. It was Hemingway who loved bullfight rings in Spain. It was Hemingway who wrote about war and wrote poetry from the time he was twelve years old.

David Bourne cannot write about what he knows he thought. *David Bourne cannot write about what he only dreams in his mind. He has—I have no mind. I am mindless.*

"Papa!" David turned his head toward the balcony, shouting.

"What!" Hemingway bellowed from the living room.

"Go to hell!"

David heard Hemingway cursing as he climbed the stairs. In only eleven stomps, he stood in the doorway, glaring at David.

"Damn you! Get up!" Hemingway shouted, crouching as he always did to do battle.

David swiveled, rising. Hemingway took a right step forward, a left, and another right, swinging his right arm so his fist would strike David's chin and render his opponent unconscious. The blow he had planned did not take place. His fist passed through David like a brook trout spawning upstream.

"I should be in Hell," Hemingway raged, "but I'm only in Kentucky!"

Chapter Twenty-seven

"God!" David shouted.

"I told you to call me Papa," Hemingway shouted.

"Papa!"

"What?"

"Can we talk?"

"I can, I don't know about you. If you want to be a writer, you have to get the grammar right. Is it about the reviews?" Hemingway asked.

"It about you, about us..."

"There is no us!" Hemingway shouted. "I'm a spirit out of my skin and you're a character off the page."

"What did you say about Dorothy Parker?" David asked.

Hemingway did not answer the question, but appeared in the doorway.

"I don't have to answer that," Hemingway said. "I'm out of here."

Hemingway disappeared.

Chapter Twenty-eight

David watched Hemingway walk across the muddy field leaving no tracks. He watched him bend forward and put two fingers on his left hand into the mud.

"Hell!" Hemingway shouted when he looked up and saw David. "And I'm not afraid of anything..."

"But I scared the shit out of you!"

"Don't put words in my mouth..."

"Because I'm not a writer?"

"Do you know who Dorothy Parker was?" Hemingway asked.

"No," David answered.

"Do you know what she said about me when she saw the photo shoot my first wife's friend did for my publicity campaign?"

"No, I don't," David said.

"She said that the photographs would distract from my work. When women saw me highlighted by the black background, hearts would quiver. I protested loudly against Dorothy Parker for her failed suicide attempts..."

"But you blew your mind out in Idaho after you'd made a name for yourself in literature."

"You are reading too many reviews. Some critics said I thought I was God, and you believed I was God," Hemingway laughed. "Why don't you leave me alone?"

"I can't. I thought you had left one time and I was worried, but I know I don't have to worry anymore. You disappear like that and I appear where you are. I have no control over it. Do you know that somebody wrote that, as long as there are the literate, there will be the Hemingway-lovers?"

"No," Hemingway said, beside David. "Let's hope that doesn't mean as long as there is a you that you will be the monkey on my back."

"What were you doing over there?"

"I was measuring deer tracks, a buck, fourteen-pointer I'd say…"

"Pointer?" David asked.

"The size of its rack—its horns," Hemingway explained.

"You can tell that by measuring its tracks?"

"I saw it cross there," Hemingway laughed. "I was remembering another hunt in Africa. Can you recall the complex relationships between the hunter, the hunted and the African natives who were essential to the ritual of their confrontation? Of course you can't!"

"Were you always in search of your manhood?" David asked.

"More often in search of womanhood," Hemingway laughed.

"But more than one critic wrote that you hated women; had a death wish and a shallow personality," David said. "Your wife, Mary, even weighed that out about you in her book..."

"Why don't you go away?"

"I can't," David said. "I don't know how."

"What else did you read about me?" Hemingway asked.

"One person wrote that you were the high priest of violence..."

"Because of the bullfights, no doubt," Hemingway said.

"Exactly," David said. "It would appear that you wrote of them with zeal..."

"I never tried to exalt what happened to the bulls and horses. I only wanted to show the reader how a matador dances with death. I wanted to write well. Is that wrong?"

"I can't say," David said.

"I can say!" Hemingway mocked David. "No matter what else happens in life violence and death are always involved," Hemingway finished his short speech then disappeared.

When David reappeared in the A-frame loft, Hemingway began to talk, pointing his finger, saying, "The Running of the Bulls is the event of the Fiesta of San Fermin. I may have been ambivalent of death and violence, but they hurt me so much toward the end that I knew my own demise was at hand. In the beginning, I made fiction around such things. My novel about bullfighting helped give the Fiesta worldwide fame. That week in July begins at eight o'clock each morning from the 7th to the 14th. Young men run in front of the bulls from their pen up and into the bullring. The run of about half a mile lasts no longer than two to three minutes unless the bulls get into the crowd or turn around. No one has to sign up anywhere to take part; you should go and just enter into the run and choose the street where you will run and try to do as best as you can. What else did those critics write about me?"

"So much I wouldn't know where to begin," David said.

"Just tell me the first thing that comes to mind!"

"One thought you were not humorous," David said.

"Mark Twain was funny," Hemingway said. "On the 15th there is a parody of the run made by some die-hards who refuse to face the fact that the Fiesta is over. They run... Hell, I'll show you."

David watched as Hemingway gathered Tomas' notebook and pencil and began to write: **David stands at the rear of the pack on Santo Domingo Street, waiting for the early-morning bus**.

"Why don't they start running?" David called, wishing he were not at the Fiesta of San Fermin, especially not in the middle of the street.

See the bus, David, Hemingway wrote, smiling.

See David run.

Run, David.

Run.

With gusto, Hemingway sang: "*A San Fermín pedimos, por ser nuestro patrón, nos guíe en el encierro dándonos su bendición*"

Chapter Twenty-nine

"I have been watching these pictures," Hemingway said, pointing at the computer that he had learned to turn on and off.

"I've seen them before," David said. "They pop up when you don't punch keys for a minute or so."

"One minute exactly," Hemingway said.

"You are not without humor," David said.

"Thank you, sir," Hemingway said. "Had a good run, did you? What can you tell me about the pictures?"

"Nothing at all," David said. "Do they mean something to you?"

David thought Hemingway would disappear when he asked him that, but he did not. He looked at the screen until the slide show of seven pictures began anew.

"The Abduction," Hemingway said. "An oil on canvas by Cézanne... 1867... His early work..."

"Was he good?"

"He was an artist's artist, obsessed with form rather than content, but he painted with one goal, to please himself. He was like I was, a brooding, complex man, given to rages, grudges, and depressions. In one thing we differed though. He had few friends. I always had friends. Just look at them around my marlin in that one. Five hundred and twelve pounds it was. I wish they wouldn't disappear so quickly. And we were different in another way. He was a recluse. I never wrote because I was bored. I went after my stories. I lived hard, I drank hard, and I was hard on women."

"He influenced you?" David asked.

"I never told people which paintings taught me perspective, but I could write paragraphs the way he painted. I used words to create landscapes like he used color to show the stolid significance he placed upon the steep slopes of Mont Sainte-Victoire. Look at this one. He studied bathers, and based this painting upon what he knew: male models, and a landmark he sketched throughout his life. Just look at how he did the trees above the men..."

"He bent them; pointed them," David said, "like a mountain."

"That's the eye you've got to train if you ever plan to be a writer. It's the poet's eye," Hemingway said. "Cézanne painted from his studio looking across the intervening valley. His work was a combination of memory, earlier studies, and sources in the art of the past; and successive views of the Mont Sainte-Victoire, his landmark formed in those trees."

"Why do you say a poet's eye when he was an artist?"

"A poet is an artist. A poet sees things others overlook," Hemingway said. "A poet sees life in everyday objects, in the flight of birds, the wings of a butterfly, or red silk poppies in bloom and captures the details on paper the way Cézanne created scenes on canvas."

"You wrote poetry..."

"All my life," Hemingway said, "even before I wrote it."

"That was not a question," David said. "I just wanted to say that I knew you wrote poetry. There's no way you could have written it before you were born."

"I grant you that, David. Every man, every woman was alive before birth except for you. You just can't understand what I meant until you write that first paragraph and it is as resonant, haunting, as a poem. Only then will you be able to contain the movement of a novel, or predict a lover's fate. Only then will you be able to transcend what you have written. Cézanne had the eye. It was an artist's eye in his hands. He achieved permanence but knew his work as only an interpretation of nature. I envied him. I used the same technique to put words on the page—where they had to be. Critics picked up on my meticulous placement and repetition of key words and images. That's how I created patterns perceptive readers could see and want more of. What I just said may not mean anything to you," Hemingway said, almost apologetically.

"It might," David said. "There's violence in *The Abduction* like I told you in the field when I said some critics saw violence as a predominant theme in your work."

"What a mouthful of a sentence," Hemingway said. "Does it suggest anything else to you besides the fact that abduction, rape, and murder were themes that tormented him?"

"Yes," David said. "The man is tan, muscular, taking what he wants. The woman is white, fainted, victim."

"Oh-h-h!" Hemingway rubbed his chin.

"I think you got your idea for Catherine, her obsession with being dark like a man, her wanting to be Peter and me her girl, from this painting."

"It took me days, day after day, hour after hour of studying his paintings in Paris to learn what I could from him. A painting is born of oil or watercolor that an artist uses. Cézanne used oil according to rules he dedicated his life to understanding. He helped make me see that nothing exists in isolation. For him things had color and they had weight. The color and weight of each affected the weight of the other. It was that insight that I put to use. Writing has words and words have weight. Writing with its mass of words and the weight of each of them combined reveals to the reader a sense of the mystery of the world. However, David, the weight of writing with its mass of words cannot reveal that which by any other name is called romance. End of lesson..."

Chapter Thirty

"I don't want to be in Spain for the Running of the Bulls," David shouted down to Hemingway when he saw the words flash across his eyelids, but he was there for the writer wrote: **A rocket goes off at the moment the bulls are let out into the street. A second rocket goes off to let everyone know that all the bulls are in the street.**

This is the moment of truth, David. The bulls run like the very devil. It is impossible to race them or even keep up with them for very long. Even I in my prime never made such athletic pretensions. The way to do it is, to start off slowly when the bulls are still a good distance behind. As they draw nearer start running like hell. Before they get too close, decide whether to hang in near them for a short time, as near as you are prepared to risk your skin, and then get out of the way as cleanly as possible. Be careful not to cross the paths of other runners. Look for a gap in the fence to slip through or jump over, or a space against the wall of the street. Enjoy the risk of running or find a safe place to watch the run from behind the fences.

"David is not ready to run with the bulls, yet," Hemingway shouted and David was back in the upstairs bedroom.

Chapter Thirty-one

At work, after reading his emails, Tomas wrote the woman, asking: **What has happened to the only other writer I know in our town?**

Tomas went up the hill to the administration building to meet with the Dean of Students, Chris Schmidt. He smiled as he thought about the joke he and Chris' wife, Rebecca had planned. Chris had told her the day she bought a Corvette and drove it home would be the day he divorced her. Tomas told her he would let her drive his Corvette home just to test her husband's resolve. He and Chris would be interviewing two college students for a secretarial position at the Upward Bound office. It was almost three hours later that Tomas returned to his office.

The woman had answered his query, writing: **I have been very busy. Today or possibly Thursday are the only times I will have for the next week.**

I should be home by 5:30 today he wrote. **If you come, bring poetry. I will read it while you read. I want to give you the books and introduce you to a couple of poets. If not today, give me a call on Thursday and tell me what time to expect you if you are not too full of one-legged turkey.**

After he had sent the email, he thought of another poet whose work he admired. He copied jpeg files from his desktop that he wanted to add to his computer's slide show.

He drove Highway 55 from Columbia to 127 without encountering any traffic in his lane. On 127, however, the curves, snaking along ridges toward Wolf Creek Dam delayed him as they did daily on his commute. It was 5:27 when he parked his Kia in the garage. He took an armload of wood from the garage into the house and built a fire. By 6:30, he knew the woman was not coming. He went upstairs and loaded the jpeg files then wrote until 9:45. He turned off the computer and went downstairs for he was tired.

He woke after midnight and went to the utility room to get his coveralls. He went outside, a brisk wind, bracing, chased sleep from his body. He felt a drop, then another, of rain or perhaps wet snow. He could feel the icy chill in the air that promised snow, if not on this night, then soon. He went to the garage and brought in as much wood as he could carry. He placed the wood on the red-glowing coals and closed the fire screen and glass doors. He sat in the swivel rocker, facing the fireplace until the fire burned with a feeble orange blaze. When the flames fanned the length of the wood, now blue with white tips, he opened the doors and let the heat chase the chill that had caused him to shiver when he stood on the patio. He removed his coveralls and went to the sofa, covering himself with a comforter. He would close the doors when the heat pump kicked on.

He woke later, glancing at the A-frame wall of glass to see if the fire had gone out. He saw flames reflected there, but he also saw the reflection of a doorway at the same height as the loft. He realized that his computer screen saver had caused the illumination. He smiled.

Chapter Thirty-two

Hemingway turned on the computer as soon as Tomas closed the kitchen door. He got up while the computer loaded and went through the bathroom to part the vertical blinds slightly. He watched Tomas enter the garage and back the Kia out. When he walked back into the bedroom, David sat in the desk chair, watching the slide show.

"Get..." Hemingway began, but did not complete his order.

"He wanted you to know he knows you are here, I think," David said.

"So now you can think?"

"I wanted to use the word **feel**, but I know I don't feel so if I know that then the knowing must be more than a feeling."

"I have to figure out what to do with you," Hemingway said, shaking his head. "How would you have me write you out of my life?"

"You left me writing at the end of the book. That's what I want to be able to do. I read one critic's explanation of how you wrote."

"And how was it that I wrote?" Hemingway asked.

"You had form that you followed."

"You mean a formula?"

"Maybe," David said, "but the critic wrote form, one where even in defeat there is victory."

"Was the critic a he or a she?"

"I can't say," David said.

"Was the comment about *The Old Man and the Sea,*" Hemingway asked, "a statement about how the sharks ate the old man's catch?"

"No," David said. "It was about *The Garden of Eden.* The book was a sensational bestseller when it was published in 1986, at least according to the critic. The critic's view was that even when my marriage was over, you gave me Marita who would inspire more writing. When Catherine burned my manuscript, you gave me hope by having me write. You made me a writer who knew none of the work would be lost."

"Just so you'll know," Hemingway shouted, "I worked sixteen fucking years on that book! Nick was an artist in it. Like you, he was married. They cut them out of it, culled too much driftwood just to make your story the book."

"Could it be that mine was a story worth telling?"

"It depends," he said, "I'd say it's possible. I worked on a book about the sea. I used parts of it to win the Pulitzer Prize one year, the Nobel Prize in Literature the next but I never meant for *The Garden of Eden* to be prostituted like they did it. I never wanted it to be just another whore!"

"Read those reviews in that yellow folder, please," David pointed toward the bed. "The one that comes to mind—I'm sorry for using that word since I'm only an extension of your mind— is the one where the reviewer said despite its weakness, its being incomplete, there is a solid flow of story. While the ending isn't typically you, it is a strong ending. The book does not harm your reputation. I don't know which ones did harm, but..."

"I'll fucking read them!" Hemingway shouted, grabbing the folder.

"I'd be proud to keep calling you Papa," David said.

Hemingway grunted and walked down the steps one at a time for he carried the open folder.

Chapter Thirty-three

"Listen to this!" Hemingway shouted from the living room then began to read: "Hemingway, one of the most acclaimed writers of the 20th century, winner of the 1954 Nobel Prize for Literature and a legend as a man, warrior, womanizer and drinker, was a writer who excelled at breaking all the rules. What rubbish. I learned the lean, spare writing style that brought me success when I was a journalist."

"I read that," David said. "I remember you were quoted saying use short sentences."

"You go back and read those rules until you know them by heart. You don't have one of those, but learn those rules. They were the best rules I ever learned for the business of writing."

"I will," David said.

"If a man ever develops any talent for the art and the craft of writing, he will write well using those simple rules."

"What about women writers?"

"Any writer!" Hemingway shouted.

"Papa?"

"What?"

"Why did you write such lousy women?"

David heard Hemingway running up the steps.

"Hold on, Papa!" David shouted as Hemingway rushed toward him. "I just asked a question. I was reading another review by a man who wrote that you did have a formula, not a form that you used to write your novels. He apparently thought you had a strange notion about sex, and that your women and men do not seem gendered at all. The men are impotent or emasculated; the women are masculine and emasculating, or, they are multi-dimensional and self-demeaning."

"And you think that's lousy?"

"I wasn't thinking," David said. "I was asking a question. If I'd been thinking, I would have remembered what I read about you being very touchy about your writing. If I were alive, I'd get a fist in the mouth every time you get pissed off at me."

"Let me have it with both barrels," Hemingway said.

"What's that mean?" David asked.

"Just tell me why my characters were lousy!"

"According to the author..."

"Being diplomatic now, aren't you?"

"The author wrote that your female characters had lost the power to form emotional attachments or shaved their heads and had bodies that were boyish."

"If you were writing that," Hemingway instructed, "I'd tell you to trim the fat off the meat."

"What?"

"Toss out unnecessary words. When you said have bodies that are boyish, you wasted words. In writing, you would say: women with boyish bodies."

"Thanks," David said. "I am a writer."

"I'm the writer," Hemingway reminded him. "I needed romance and adventure and I wrote about the women I needed. I was accused of portraying men who dominated passive women."

"Not always," David reminded him. "I read where you created pseudo-masculine women, impotent men, but you could not put your characters together in a meaningful and fruitful relationship. Why was that?"

"I can't take any more of your analyzing right now. But put this tidbit of information where you will always remember it. In fact, I'm going to write it. It seems you make memories about things I write."

"I want to read everything you ever wrote," David said.

Hemingway looked at David and grinned. He began to write: **David Bourne was never a Hemingway tough guy. He never thought of himself as god, a masculine creative force dominating and containing feminine creation. He never knew the happiness of the Garden that men have always been doomed to lose.**

"Why did you say I was not ready for the running of the bulls?" David asked.

"Because you have no life in you," Hemingway said. "I was experimenting with something when I wrote you back to Spain."

"Just like you did now?"

"Yes, David…"

"I have all the life you gave me. When can you write more of it into me?" David asked.

Hemingway said, "I can't tell you."

"When will you tell me?"

"When I can write it," Hemingway answered, "you'll know. You have to understand something here. You're asking me to write something I never wrote before…"

"And what would that be?" David asked.

Hemingway replied, "a happy ending."

Chapter Thirty-four

Tomas saw the book on the bed as soon as he entered. The brown covers of the Modern Library edition of *Camille* that he had placed in the cherry bookcase against the chimney lay against the pillow, but not on it. He picked up the book with his left hand and flipped it over. Page 197 was turned down and one sentence was underlined in black ink. He read quickly: **Love always makes a man better, no matter what woman inspires it.**

Tomas closed the book and walked onto the landing. As he started to put the book in the space on the top shelf where it had been removed he saw the ragged end of a white piece of paper, snow white against the aging yellow pages of the book. He pulled the strip of paper from the book and read the words: **When you start to live outside yourself, it's all dangerous**. He put the note inside the book then placed the book on the shelf.

He went to the computer, but he did not turn it on. Trusting his first thought, he told himself the words did not come from *Camille*. He turned his head quickly, his peripheral vision having caught something moving right to left across the landing. He got up. When he got to the doorway, he turned on the dining room light. There was no one on the steps.

Chapter Thirty-five

"Why did you do that?" David asked the next morning when Tomas closed the kitchen door.

"I'm telling him he did best when he let the first woman go. She is a woman who cannot do well by him. A woman can break a man like snapping a bone. When he heals afterward, he is stronger at the breaks," Hemingway answered.

"When he went out to get firewood this morning, I read what you wrote on that paper and left in the book. I didn't read the words to mean that."

"What did you take them to mean?"

"They helped me understand why I can't write. I'm trying to go outside myself to find words."

Hemingway looked at David so long that David wanted him to disappear.

"I always wrote on the principal of the iceberg. On the back cover of his novel he wrote that the truth is what is unwritten. That is like my iceberg theory. All good writing has one thing in common—words are clearer when the eye sees them. He did not run from what I wrote," Hemingway explained.

"You also wrote about the second woman," David said.

"Women can be a necessary evil, inflicting pain on men. She does not show evil like a cat's eye. I always tried simply to write the best I could. I know he sees a writer in her. She doesn't see that yet or feel it. He has the good intentions of a teacher, a mentor. I was like that with young writers. I have not forgotten you either, David. I never liked to write like God, but you have me thinking that way now."

"Do you think he will understand what it is you want him to do?"

"He will think about the words until he feels something. I wouldn't blame him if he ignored them since they came from a man who killed himself," Hemingway said.

"I'm reading those articles now," David said.

'Don't ask me anything!" Hemingway shouted.

Chapter Thirty-six

When Tomas closed the kitchen door the day after Thanksgiving, he thought about the woman who did not come. He also thought about the telephone. At 1:01 in the morning, it rang once. He did not sleep after that, having those fears one gets when a telephone rings so late.

Thinking about the woman relieved his fear. She wrote: **possibly Thursday,** in her email. He smiled, thinking Thanksgiving had not been the Thursday of possibly.

He got in the Kia and drove toward Lindsey. As he drove he thought. Some thoughts were about the woman. Many were about the novel he planned to write. She had promised to help him with it. In an email he had told her he wanted to write a strong woman, one a man could both desire and appreciate. Rather than make up everything, he had hoped to be able to use her as the model for his female lead, a woman wanting to write, but finding life with its tragedies and glimmers of loving, of living, and of death to be so time intensive, she was not taking time for the writing of words. She was a woman alive, life ebbing from her more than anything else. Perhaps he should not have asked for her assistance. *If she does not return*, he decided: *I will write about wanting her to help me—about me wanting to help her with her work. At least, doing that will keep the narrative from being a work about men without women.* What he hoped to avoid in the new work was writing that a female reader could not read without having to assume a masculine persona.

He remembered a conversation that he had with Emily about Hemingway and about men who act like boys when a good-looking female enters a room. She had said: *the more I am around men, the less I understand them. I am attracted to men like Picasso and Hemingway because they misbehave. They are crude, but there is something appealing about their crudity. It must be the male mind. I like to visit it, but I wouldn't want to live there.*

When he walked down the hall toward his office, he realized that someone had been inside. The door was partially closed. He always kept it fully open. The old fears he would have had, the ones he wrote about in his last novel, did not overtake him. He pushed the door against the left wall and surveyed the room. No one had shuffled his piles of projects.

He checked his email. There were no new messages from his contacts or Lindsey Wilson College staff—only three *spams* he deleted without opening.

He waited for Lucy and Mannie, two international students. He had volunteered to be the host family for Lucy, a volleyball player from Kenya, and for Carl and Carlos, twins from the

Grand Caymans, both of whom ran track for the college. Mannie was also from Kenya. He ran track and played soccer. Lucy and Mannie worked as tutors for high school students. Tomas was the federal program director.

He had asked the four students to go home with him for Thanksgiving but they had made other plans. He asked Lucy and Mannie to go with him to Bowling Green for a day after Thanksgiving meal and they had been eager to do that. He was beginning to think, however, that they had changed their mind. They were fashionably late.

As he looked down the hallway toward the side entrance, the one he and his staff always used, he saw Mannie. He got up, walked around his desk, and met the student at the door.

"I was at Wal-Mart," Mannie said. "I ran here. Where is Lucy?"

"She's not here," Tomas said.

"Do you have a phone I can use?"

"There," Tomas pointed toward Madonna's, the assistant director and counselor's, desk.

"Do I dial...?"

"Only the last four numbers," Tomas said.

Mannie dialed and waited. He began to speak Swahili then put down the phone.

"She was waiting for me. She will come at once. How is Madonna?"

"Call her back," Tomas said before answering. "Tell her we will pick her up there. Madonna's had her surgery. She should be able to come back to work soon."

Mannie dialed Lucy's extension. She had not left, he told Tomas.

"Are you ready?" Tomas asked, opening the door.

When Tomas drove up the hill toward the administration building on the right, the president's house on the left, Mannie pointed toward a student, sitting on the sidewalk, tying his running shoe.

"He is the reason I was late," Mannie said. "He stopped me and we talked."

"It is okay," Tomas said.

"Do they have a good mall in this Bowling Green?"

"Do you want to buy something?" Tomas asked.

"I want to find a store with men's goods," Mannie said.

"We can do that."

Tomas drove to Lucy's apartment and she came to the Kia and got into the back seat behind him.

"Do you have enough room?" Tomas asked.

"No," she answered. "I can't sit behind him, but I can turn around and lean back."

Tomas drove from the college campus to the parkway. When he entered the interstate from the ramp and began to cruise, Lucy tapped Mannie on the shoulder. Tomas heard her asked him to play music.

"There are CD's in the pocket there," Tomas said, pointing.

Mannie took out three.

"Not that one," Lucy said. "The red case or the other, Lee Ann Womack, the Mississippi Girl, I was looking at hers at Wal-Mart."

Mannie chose **Alabama** and leaned back as *Back Home* played.

"Country this," Mannie said. "Country that. It's all country."

"It's country music," Tomas said. "Whose country though?"

Mannie laughed and began to speak Swahili. Lucy laughed and answered him in their language. They talked at length, with Tomas listening. He had always been a good listener, learning by listening to every word. Although he did not understand them, he loved the sounds the words made, almost melodious like birds singing.

"I think the music is a lullaby for him," Lucy called from the back seat.

"It was," Tomas said, glancing at Mannie, asleep then looking into the rear view mirror at Lucy's eyes, dark, bright, full of life.

Mannie slept. Tomas drove. Lucy sang the words she knew of each song, sang silently, her lips keeping the beat. Soon Lucy put her head against the seat and the door and Tomas drove in silence. When he drove past Glasgow, Lucy spoke.

"May we eat at the place where we ate when you brought us to the bus station?"

"Sure," Tomas said.

"I liked that place. The food was good."

When Tomas turned off Interstate 65 toward the mall, Lucy was awake. Mannie was sleeping. Lucy began to shake him. He spoke without opening his eyes.

"Wasn't that food great!" Tomas exclaimed. "You missed it, Mannie. We're on our way back to Columbia."

Mannie opened his eyes when Tomas turned left at the entrance to Greenwood Mall. Mannie and Lucy sparred in Swahili while Tomas drove, making his way slowly toward the Longhorn restaurant.

When Tomas parked, Mannie said," It's not far to Bowling Green."

"Not when you're asleep," Tomas said.

"I was tired from running back from Wal-Mart," Mannie said.

In the restaurant when the waitress came to get their drink orders, Mannie asked, "do you have juices?"

"Sure," she said. "Orange, cranberry..."

"Do you have pineapple?" he asked.

"Yes we do," she answered.

"That's my favorite."

"What will you have, mam?" she asked Lucy.

"Water..."

"Water," Mannie chimed.

"And you, sir?" she asked Tomas.

"Water with lemon," Tomas answered.

Mannie tucked his chin, his lips miming the words: *water with lemon?*

"Very well, sir," the waitress said. "I'll bring those right out."

"I add sugar and make lemonade," Tomas said.

Mannie nodded.

Before the waitress returned, Mannie began to drink, emptying the glass.

"Running made me thirsty," he said.

"Are you ready to order," the waitress asked when she returned.

"Why is my glass smaller than theirs?" Mannie asked her.

"Yours came from the bar," she said. "That's where we keep the pineapple juice."

"May I have a refill?" Mannie asked.

"Certainly," she said, leaving them, returning shortly with another glass of juice and a small loaf of bread.

"Is that good?" Mannie asked.

"It's good stuff," she said and took their orders.

Lucy cut the small loaf into four slices. They ate the bread. While they waited for their food, Mannie emptied his glass for the second time.

When the waitress returned, she placed the food on the table and looked at Mannie's glass.

"They only allow one refill of juice," she said before Mannie could ask for another.

Tomas motioned for her.

"It's okay to keep it running?" she asked to make sure she understood what Tomas' gesturing had meant.

"A tab," Tomas said. "They are from Kenya. They can't go home for Thanksgiving. I'm their host family..."

"He's my father," Mannie said. "Don't you think we look alike?"

"He is my son and Lucy is my daughter," Tomas said. "This is their Thanksgiving dinner the day after..."

"Thank you for having us," Mannie said to the waitress.

She smiled.

"It's our pleasure," she said.

"May we have another loaf of bread?" Tomas asked.

"Certainly," she said.

"They put too much ice in it," Mannie said.

When she brought the juice and the breadboard, Lucy began to cut the end nearest her. Mannie spoke.

"Do you know what he was saying?" Lucy asked.

"No," Tomas said.

"He said for me to cut the other end off for you and he would eat the big middle."

Tomas smiled.

Lucy cut the bread into four slices.

"He was just kidding," she said.

"How far is it from here to Columbia?" Mannie asked.

"Seventy-five or eighty miles from where we are now," Tomas said.

"I could run that in a day," Mannie said.

"Have you saved room for dessert?" the waitress asked when they had finished eating.

Mannie looked at Tomas, rubbing his stomach.

"I think he's full," Tomas laughed, and gave the waitress a hundred dollars.

"I drank too much juice," Mannie said, smiling.

"For you," Tomas said, tipping the waitress when she came back with his change.

"And for you," she said, handing him a gift card. "You must use it by the thirteenth of December."

"Thanks you so much," Tomas said.

When Tomas backed from the parking space, Mannie looked toward the restaurant.

"She liked us," Mannie said. "She came out to see us off."

"She did like us," Tomas said.

"That's not her," Lucy said.

"It is her!" Mannie exclaimed.

Tomas looked toward the entrance. The waitress was not the one who had served them.

"If that's the same one," Tomas said, "she got pregnant in a hurry."

"Mannie is fast like that," Lucy laughed.

Tomas drove from the restaurant parking lot to the mall. There were no empty parking spaces.

"This is the biggest shopping day of the year all across America," Tomas said. "We may not find a parking space."

"Why is that?" Mannie asked.

"The shops run sales that are not sales and shoppers believe them—flock in to find bargains."

"I like this country music," Mannie said, listening to the CD. "I like their accent when they sing."

The third time through the lots Mannie spotted a car backing from a space behind them.

"If I could back up," Tomas said. "We'd get that."

A truck approached.

"He will get it," Lucy said.

Tomas turned right at the stop sign, speeding to the end of the street, turning right ahead of another pick-up and right into the lane where the empty space was located.

"They're going to get it," Mannie said.

Tomas drove quickly, turning into the space while the car in question turned right toward them.

Inside the mall, Mannie looked at jeans displayed outside Abercrombie & Fitch.

"I don't like them," he said. "They look old. That is not my fashion. I want a new look."

"Let's go back the way we came," Tomas said. "We can find some there."

"Look!" Lucy shouted.

Tomas looked ahead. William Luckey, Lindsey Wilson College President, walked toward them, grinning.

"What are you doing here?" he asked Lucy.

Lucy did not answer.

"I'm Lucy's host family," Tomas said. "I brought them today for Thanksgiving dinner and for shopping."

"That's great," President Luckey said. "I was in your office last night. I was showing it to some friends, telling them how we lived there."

"I noticed," Tomas said, "but it's fine."

"Good to see you," he said. "Enjoy the rest of your trip."

"What was he doing here?" Lucy asked.

"He probably came shopping with his family and is walking around the mall to get his exercise in," Tomas said. "He was wearing his athletic clothes."

"That's what he was doing," Lucy said.

"Do they have men's goods in here?" Mannie asked when Lucy entered a store.

"There in the back," Tomas pointed.

Mannie went to the far right corner and began to look at the different styles of jeans.

"What size do you wear?" Tomas asked.

"At least this long," Mannie said, holding the jeans against his waist.

"What is your waist size?"

"I don't know," Mannie said.

Tomas picked up a pair of jeans in his size.

"Put your arm like this," he instructed. "The waist should be the size of your arm from the elbow to the wrist like this…"

"If that is right, these are too big," Mannie said.

"Find a pair that fits your arm like I showed you. Take them into the fitting room and see if I am right."

Mannie found a pair. He went into the fitting room and changed. When he looked over the door, Tomas could tell he was not pleased.

"How did that work?" Tomas asked.

"I have learned something," Mannie said. "They are just right around but the legs are too tight at the bottom."

"All our styles are like that," the salesman who had joined them said.

"We can try Old Navy," Lucy said.

When they went into Old Navy, Tomas saw a rack of fake snakeskin jackets to their right. Above the jacket, a sign with red letters promised 50% off.

"Come with me," Tomas said. "I want to explain something for you, Lucy. See this jacket. It is on sale."

"50% off," she smiled. "A good price..."

"See this jacket?" Tomas asked. "If you buy it, look."

He measured the space between the jacket and the floor and turned toward Lucy. This is the 50% that is off. You pay 100% for the jacket, but you have nothing to wear with it. What will people think of you if you wear this outfit, a jacket only with nothing on the 50% of you that is below?"

The question embarrassed Lucy and she rushed off.

Chapter Thirty-seven

"Have you seen the new pictures he put on the screen last night?" David shouted.

"No!" Hemingway shouted in return. "What kind of pictures?"

"Of you, you and women, one of a bullfight..."

Hemingway appeared behind David, watching, waiting.

"There," David pointed.

"That's the arena, but it's not an actual bullfight. The bull has rubber tipped horns. They let young men and want to be matadors like me get in the ring with bulls like that."

"Are you in there?"

"That's me with the cape," Hemingway said.

"In front of the bull?"

"That's where the action is," Hemingway said. "If Antonio was in the ring fighting when I was in Spain, I would go beforehand and actually look at the bulls. I learned how the other matadors fought bulls by talking to them, but I learned what bullfighting is by watching Antonio in the ring, orchestrating every move."

"You once said never to confuse motion for action," David said.

"You almost got it right," Hemingway said. "What I actually said was never mistake motion for action."

"Papa?"

"What, David?"

"I want to be a writer more than anything. I still can't do it."

"I know and I'm sorry you can't. There are some things, which cannot be learned quickly, and writing is one of them. It was such a simple thing for me, but I learned it by trial and error, I taught myself to write prose. I discovered that writing is only a transaction between writer and reader. It is about being human all the time... I shouldn't have said that. To see you this way reminds me of how it was in the end."

"When you killed yourself?"

"My best friends said that I'd done everything, I'd written everything. Most of them agreed that the last great thing I wrote was *The Old Man and the Sea*."

"I'm glad they printed *The Garden of Eden.*"

"I am too, David," Hemingway said, "but only for your sake. Words were the only heritage I had to leave that mattered."

"You wrote that there is no friend as loyal as a book..."

"I did," Hemingway said. "I'm going to finish your story soon."

"How?"

"I'm still not sure. It is the most difficult work I have ever faced. I keep waiting for that instant of realization when I discover hidden dimensions of truth. Then I will write life into you. It takes that..."

"You've told me that," David interrupted.

"A man has to have life to know what is worthy in it. The little things must be written with great conviction."

"Is that how you wrote, Papa?"

"When I wrote well," he answered. "The quality of my later fiction was affected by my health. There were those two plane crashes in Africa, particularly the one that fractured my skull. Near the end, they tricked me."

"Who did?"

"My wife and doctor," he said. "They began to do twice-weekly electroshock treatments at the Mayo Clinic."

"I read where you got sick while on a hunting trip near Sun Valley, Idaho. That's why they admitted you. The article reported your illness was not serious, no surgery required."

"It was surgery nonetheless. I had an incredible memory. They took it. The words never came back after those treatments. Life, you will learn when you have it, David, is filled with tensions; yet, peopled by good and bad intentions," Hemingway said.

"Give me life like you had," David begged. "Let me know romance and physical activity so I can get the writing done."

"I gave you that in the book, David. If that's all it takes to make you happy, I can finish it right now. Let me have your chair!"

David stood, moving left toward the wall while Hemingway sat down.

"What are you going to write?" David asked, his voice a tremor of excitement.

"You can read it as it comes," Hemingway said, writing: **when David woke from his dream and felt Marita's breast against his** bare, tan chest, he was happy. He was happy with the woman in his bed—happy his work came out of him with an ease some writers never experience. He no longer wrote slowly, painstakingly. He had moved beyond the offering and withdrawing of emotion in his fiction. His work reflected the essential rhythms of his life, his craft and art. He had finished his fifth novel late in the afternoon then they made love into the early hours of morning.

Critics had written glowing reviews about his fourth book, positive statements, suggesting he had been born to write. They did not know he was only observing life and recording it faithfully as he saw it.

"You aren't writing by your rules," David said, realizing that something—his anger perhaps kept him in the loft with Hemingway rather than putting him in the woman's bed.

"I'm not leaving here this time," David said. "Your sentences are not true—not what I want..."

David touched Marita and fell asleep holding her. He began to dream the same dream. In his dream, David drifted within an abyss, falling toward nada in his search for meaning. He had learned how to write honestly but he had not learned how to face death.

"Don't kill me off," David said, returning very much afraid of where the writer was going with his story. "You promised to give me life. I don't want to die before I have lived long enough to cheat death like you did."

"You were in bed with a woman. You could touch her, kiss her, and fuck her. What more of life could you want?"

"You were in that bed," David said. "I was not. I know Marita was part of your life, not mine. She was docile. The book reflects your life, the lives of your women, women you loved and hated. They were your wives, your lovers, and your closet longings. They are dead to me. Give me life as you promised. I don't want to die in an instant."

"Every story, if it goes on long enough, ends in death, David."

"Just keep that from me for a while. I want to find a woman like the second woman who came here. You had your infatuation with silent film star Mae Marsh. Don't deny me mine. I want to make my own mistakes."

"Spoken like the child you are, David. I think you're reading too much about me. Mae Marsh, yes, yes..."

"I want to read it all, not just the snippets the man brings home."

"You might detest me then. For your information, I would choose the first woman," Hemingway said. "She uses her female body..."

"So that's how you would justify using hers?"

"Some questions are their own answers," Hemingway said.

"Is that a cliché?" David asked.

"It could be."

"Then you're breaking your rules again. I don't want to be in your book any longer than it takes for you to give me life. I don't like your women. I don't want to be your alter ego. I want to know what a woman's breast feels like against my skin, but I want to choose her. I don't want to be in love with two women at once. I want to write one of your true sentences!"

Hemingway did not speak at one then said, "Ashley... He's writing like me and the red head is like Ashley—like I wrote her..."

David watched him for a moment.

"Who is this woman?"

"Pauline Pfeiffer, my second wife. You cut me with your words, David, as does that picture. I had forgotten the hell it was telling myself I loved the two of them the same, Pauline and

Hadley. That picture was made on her uncle's boat. This picture you see now is Hadley..."

"Your first wife," David said.

"Hadley with one of her pets... When women get neglected by their men, they get pets."

"You took that from one of your stories..."

"No, David," Hemingway said. "I put those words in my work."

"I don't care for Cézanne's bathers," David said when the slide show continued. "They are restrained, impersonal, and remote like I am now."

"I suppose you like Renoir's sensuous girls in the water, David, or the two women at a café," Hemingway stated.

"Did you use those two for Catherine and Marita?" David asked.

"Hell no!" Hemingway cursed. "They're not my type. I wanted my girls to be pals. Shit, I preferred women who looked like boys not those over-feminine women Renoir painted."

"Look at the black and white prints the man put on the bed," David said.

Hemingway got up.

"Next to *A Farewell to Arms,*" David directed.

Hemingway picked up the page Tomas had printed on a laser printer that could not reproduce the colors Renoir had chosen to capture the moment the two women embraced, their fingers in the background intimate, telling their story better than their faces or one woman's unseen lips against the other's cheek.

"The one on the left reminds me of Hadley," Hemingway said. "Maybe subconsciously I thought about this when I wrote *The Garden of Eden.* Though I'd rather believe I was having good luck, writing better than a man should."

"Who is that?"

"Martha Gellhorn, my third wife," Hemingway said.

"She has long hair..."

"She stayed pissed off at me," he said. "She accused me of dragging her around like a wet rag. She was the only one of my wives that divorced me. Before you ask, that is my fourth wife, Mary Walsh..."

"She wrote that you hated women and was the one who tricked you."

"Yes," Hemingway whispered, " zapped writing from my memory. Left me, like you are, David, unable to write a word..."

"I want you to set me free," David said.

"I just can't do it like that. Life's too dangerous. You want to be alive and in love, but you have no clue as to the real cost of both."

"But I want to fish. I want to drive the Bugatti again," David said.

"You wouldn't recognize a Bugatti if you saw one."

"Would, too," David returned. "There's a white one in the garage."

"Let's go!" Hemingway ordered.

"Where, Papa?"

"To the car..."

Chapter Thirty-eight

Tomas emailed the woman on Monday: *I hope you had an enjoyable Thanksgiving...*

She wrote back: *I'm still planning to come see you within the next few days...*

Tomas had a few minutes to reflect before he and Chris Schmidt would meet to discuss the applicants for the secretary's position with the Lindsey's federal program.

The telephone he did not have had not rung anymore. He found himself wishing he could have somehow picked up the receiver and said something, anything...

He had not decided on a name for the woman, one to be used in the novel. His thought was to disguise her, but not so thinly that the readers in their rural community would know her. He imagined how they would ask who she was—would ask him, and ask each other. He liked the idea that they would discuss the book while trying to discover her. In doing so, a few might suspect first one woman then another.

As he thought, he realized how like a glowworm consciousness is. The unknown subconscious he equated with darkness, with dreams, with the projections of hate or of love. It had taken a tornado to cause him to trust both his conscious and unconscious mind. When the house he was in exploded, fracturing his lower spine, he told himself that the thick air, the millions of pieces of particles in the black swirling cloud, were singing his death song, words roaring through his brain but so incomprehensible, although the song was accompanied by a train's angry rush through a tunnel that song could not overpower his inner voice. His unconscious mind told him to crawl into the fireplace—told him it was not time to die. He listened. He lived.

Common sense is the god within our heads who keeps our wildest dreams and our tenderness, our desires confined to our imaginations he thought. As he crawled into the fireplace, the voice, promising him that he would emerge was his own, but it was also the voice of a stranger. The chimney withstood the fury.

Blood red... he thought. *Fire red, the color that burns along the veins, giving brightness to the night as surely as the feeble glow of a larva, the color of life itself, red... The gemstone that brings red to vivid life is the ruby.*

And he thought: *the woman's car of choice is a red Corvette. Her birth month, July, her traditional genuine birthstone, ruby, one of the world's most revered gemstones and also one of the rarest...* He realized that his thoughts were details he could put into the book.

The red hue of ruby, fiery and romantic draws attention. Symbolically, a ruby shouts I am passion, look at me, and see my drop-dead glamour my femininity.

"My idle mind," he said aloud, laughing, wondering how many of those words, the barrage that rushed from his random thoughts, he would remember when it came time to write them.

Chapter Thirty-nine

"Look for the name of the car," Hemingway told David. "This is not a Bugatti. I don't know what it is, but it is not a Bugatti."

"Where will I find the name?" David asked.

Hemingway looked through the door into the car. There were no instruments on the dash.

"There should be an emblem on it somewhere," Hemingway said.

"I've found it," David said, reading the sticker on the right, rear window: **Travis Tritt, NHRA...**

"That's fitting," Hemingway chuckled. "This is a hot rod, a man's car. I saw a lever on the back. Go move it from off to on..."

"Got it!" David shouted from the rear of the car.

"Come on!" Hemingway shouted. "Get in!"

"But I want to drive it!" David protested, opening the passenger door. "Where do I sit?"

"Hunker down in the floor board," Hemingway said. "I'll start it and back it out.

You can watch me, see what I do, and then I'll let you drive."

Hemingway flipped every toggle switch he saw on the metal board, mounted beneath the tachometer and in front of the gearshift. When he pushed the ignition button and tapped the gas pedal, the car started, roaring from the open headers beneath the doors on both sides. He shifted into reverse and let the car pull itself backward into the driveway. He stopped, shifted into park, and got out. When he opened the door on the passenger's side, David had already settled into the driver's seat.

"I like the sound of this **Travis Tritt NHRA**," David said. "I know how to use the brake. Hold on! Here we go!"

But David kept his left foot on the brake pedal even as he pushed his right foot down on the gas pedal. The car sat still, tires squalling, and the black smoke rolling out of the rear quarters rose up into a light west breeze and filled the inside of the race car.

"Pick up your left foot!" Hemingway shouted.

When David removed his foot, the car shot backward twenty yards before Hemingway could reach the kill switch.

"Let me have it!" Hemingway shouted. "Look what you did to the road!"

"I'm putting it back!" David yelled, flipping the toggle and pushing the ignition button the way he had seen Hemingway do.

"Squeeze that lever on the gear shift." Hemingway yelled back. "Shift forward to park or it won't start."

David shifted into park and started the engine. As it roared, he shifted again and tromped the gas pedal. With tires melting asphalt, the car bolted toward the house until Hemingway got his left hand on the steering wheel and found the kill switch with his right thumb. David stomped the brake when Hemingway steered the car into the garage. Hemingway passed through the windshield, slid the length of the hood, and landed on his back in the garage floor.

David rushed toward Hemingway, laughing, "That **Travis Tritt NHRA** is one wild ride. I like this car better than any Bugatti I never knew. Let's do it again!"

Hemingway disappeared.

Tomas saw the black tire marks on the driveway when he got home. He shook his head, thinking his brother-in-law, the owner of the dragster, had been the culprit. He parked the Kia in the Garage and walked to the A-frame.

Chapter Forty

"Are you still mad at me?" David called from the loft bedroom.

"What do you want, David?"

"I want to talk to the man who was charming, witty, and romantic when he was sober," David answered.

Hemingway appeared, looking over David's shoulder as the slide show changed from a painting of Tomas' father to a shot of him kicking a can.

"I like you in that picture," David said. "I like the snow. How does it feel?"

"It was a wet snow," Hemingway said, "the kind I always enjoyed. The air was still warm that day. The ground was warm, melting the snow before dark, I believe."

"What are you doing with that gun?" David asked.

"That was in Spain," Hemingway said. "I was at the front, helping the man with his gun. It had jammed. I liked the front lines where the fighting was fierce and a man's bravery could not be questioned. I went there to get away from Hadley. Martha followed me. If I can give you life, David, there's something I want you to remember always."

"What?"

"Women and money can do a man in. Say it for me!"

"Women and money can do a man in..."

"Martha learned from me and became one of the best war correspondent during World War Two. I would tell her now that I am sorry I got peeved at her for that," Hemingway lamented. "I was hard on anyone whose star was rising."

"I don't know what that means, but I like the elephant on the river bank," David pointed. "And the two elephants in this picture, but I don't like the next one. You look so pleased with yourself posing with that dead leopard. I read where you said you like killing animals because you were giving them the gift of death..."

"John James Audubon was a famous naturalist and painter of exotic birds. His work glorified birds. When he discovered a new bird specimen, he killed it, ran wires through its body, and posed it. Some people will find it strange to learn that Audubon loved shooting birds. He gave them the gift of death in life in order to give them a new life in his paintings.

Writing is like that. How did you know it was a leopard?"

"The border in the bathroom has them on it." David said. "I heard Tomas say, one morning, *good morning leopard—good morning elephant—good morning zebra—good morning giraffe*. When he went to work, I went in there and saw that the repeating pattern was indeed the cat, the long tusks, the black and white and the long neck."

"Know this, David, if a story goes on long enough it ends in death."

"You said that already," David reminded him.

"So I did, David. So I did... Hunting is one of man's oldest rituals, the stuff of legends and myths."

"Cézanne's bathers," David said.

"And what do you remember about it?"

"The mountain formed by the trees. That you created your landscapes the way he painted... That I need to develop a poet's eye..."

"I'm proud of you, son," Hemingway said. "I made it clear to my readers that a writer who stares into the soul and brings back what he sees is a hunter. Creating art is as much a matter of life and death as it was with the shooting of that leopard. Someone else killed it. I wouldn't let them print it until I had killed my own leopard in the traditional way with a spear. It took six shots from a shotgun to give it the gift of death. This picture of me at my writing table in Africa, I have to say, lets you see how I looked after I'd gone into myself all those years. In it, I am a man grown old before my time."

"The bullfight is next," David said. "See!"

"You've got them memorized, haven't you?"

"Yes," David admitted. "Is that really you in front of the bull?"

"Do you think I lie?"

"The last article I read said you did about many things. The author said you got caught up in them and your writing suffered..."

Hemingway disappeared.

"Come back, please," David begged.

"I certainly could outbox, out fish, outhunt, out drink, and out screw you!" Hemingway shouted.

"But I am you," David said, "and I want to be me. I want to box. I want to fish. I want to give animals your gift of death. I want to drink. Tell me what it means to screw..."

Hemingway did not answer at once. David turned the chair so he was facing him.

"If you know what making love is..."

"I don't," David said. "In *The Garden of Eden* you had us making love, eating, making love... Had me with two women, but I've never made love. Tell me what that is, too."

"Making love and screwing is the way a man gets inside a woman," Hemingway said. "When the first woman came here, they screwed. You saw what they did."

"I was under the bed, Papa" David reminded him. "I didn't see anything."

"When you can't see, David, you have to depend on your other senses. Can you feel?"

"Not with a mind," David said. "Not with skin. I didn't feel the squirrel you made me skin. And you do lie. You dropped it in the fire. We never ate it. I thought you were God and I lied when I said it was good."

"Sometimes details are no matter, David. Take us for example... I can't pin down the mystery of how you came to be. It's impossible for you to be here, but you are. As for me, of course I can't eat. I don't have a body. I have to draw energy from other sources. Sometimes I draw it from electromagnetic fields, electricity, but I can also draw it from the air. That's why I was fishing. The air was pure, the water, clean and cold. The only hints of man were the high voltage lines overhead, transmission lines. I was bathing in the flow of energy. I could move things. Maybe I pulled you there. I was thinking about all the times I wrote about fishing, even that scene in Spain where you catch the big one. It was too big for you and Catherine to eat..."

"But I want to feel hunger and I've wanted to feel the warmth of a woman from the time you asked me about that feeling."

"For us, David, time has no meaning. You can hear," Hemingway said. "What did it sound like when you were under the bed?"

"Like the bed was going to fall," David laughed. "The man was silent. The woman made sounds and said: *when you do it like that, it makes me so horny.*"

"He was thinking. She was feeling."

"Did he go into her?"

"Yes, David..."

"Did she grow horns like the bull?"

"David, David!" Hemingway laughed excitedly. "You are such an innocent child."

"But when he came out of her, he was not like the hunter you talked about coming out of his soul, so it was not the end of the story." David said. "It was not the tragedy you call death?"

"Maybe you should stop planning, David. You have no future. Your past is a book. Let's wait to see if I can give you life," Hemingway said. "Some things are best if a woman shows you. You will never forget the first feel of a woman nor your last. I hope I can give you a chance to experience that and then you will understand the excitement of it forever."

"That's Pauline with you," David said. "She was rich."

"Yes, David," Hemingway said, "she was. I claimed to be unaffected by her family's wealth, but I was not writing enough or well enough in her world. The war in Spain gave me a way out."

"Money and women," David said.

"Good, David," Hemingway smiled. "Never add to your misery by surrounding yourself with the idle rich. There was such peril in that for me."

"What is misery?"

"Your wanting life makes me miserable..."

"Because you can't give me that," David said. "I am misery."

"I'm not going to talk anymore, David," Hemingway said. "I've got to think for a while."

"One more picture," David pleaded.

"One more," Hemingway agreed. "The marlin!"

"Don't look at the fish. Look at the only girl in the picture..."

"What about her?"

"Look at her face. Is that a ghost coming out of her?"

"I never noticed that before," Hemingway said. "Strange. Could be... or the photographer... or the developer ... or something..."

"Who is that woman?" David asked, pointing. "You appear to be talking to her. She rests her chin on her hands, her hands on the chair. She is deep in thought about something."

"That's Adriana Ivancich," Hemingway answered, his voice, eager, almost proud. "That picture was taken at my home in Cuba. I met her in Italy in 1948. She took my heart."

"Did you get inside her?"

"I flirted with her."

"Flirted?" David asked. "What is that?"

"I wanted her for several years..."

"Wanted to get inside her?"

"Yes, David, but I—we—she was in my life when I needed a lift. Our relationship was platonic...?

"What does that mean?

"It's a term named after Plato, a Greek philosopher, who once said that people in the beginning were joined back to back, man joined with man or a man and a woman welded together or two women molded. They could not make love or screw, but they could be friends, companions. Adriana put a fire back in me. Whatever we did together in our relationship became the book, *Across the River and into the Trees*. She was my favorite companion in those days. She lifted my spirits a second time and I wrote *The Old Man and the Sea*. I fell in love with her."

"You fell in love with her, but you didn't get inside her. It sounds like she went into you..."

"Yes, she did, but..."

"How did Plato say people came apart?"

"He told the other gods what to do and they separated them."

"Gods?" David asked. "There's more than one?"

"In Plato's time people had gods for everything. Maybe he said Zeus cut them apart... I can't remember..."

"I wish you had been God," David said. "You could have breathed life into me..."

Hemingway did not say what he was thinking.

"Who is the nurse?"

"My first love," Hemingway said. "My eyesight was so bad here," Hemingway, pointed at his left eye, "that I couldn't get in a regular Army unit. I joined an ambulance unit. I could be a volunteer in the Italian army. An Austrian mortar round put my legs out of commission. They gave me a medal, but the best part of all that carnage was meeting her."

"Her name was Agnes," David said, standing. "I read where she was Catherine in this book."

"Yes, she was. I never got inside her."

"But you wanted to..."

"Some women put limits on their physical closeness. They are not submissive to or fulfilled by the men in their lives. She crushed me when she married that Italian officer."

"Look!" David said as two pictures fell from the book.

Hemingway stooped to retrieve them.

"Pisa," he said, holding the picture so David could view it. "The leaning tower..."

"The men are joined at the side," David remarked.

Hemingway smiled.

"In war, soldiers get close after they have been to the front and killed their enemies. The man on the left is in the picture on the wall above the sofa. He's dead..."

"How do you know that? Can you see it in his face the way I see the ghost coming out of the girl?"

"His flag is in the bedroom in a display case along with another picture of him in Italy. When a soldier dies, the family gets a flag from the military. It goes to the oldest son or to the father if the soldier is a son."

David took the picture. After he looked at it, he studied Hemingway.

"What?" Hemingway asked... "What is it!"

"You don't see it, Papa?"

"See what?"

"The man on the left is leaning like the tower. They aren't joined at the side..."

"Your eye is getting good," Hemingway beamed. "He is devilish, that one..."

David went to the landing and returned with two books.

"Read this," David said, opening the book, *Citizen Soldiers,* to page 106.

"That's the way it was," Hemingway said. "Paris was overrun by reporters and I led them..."

"I read where a critic said you never led the liberation into Paris...said that was a lie... just one more embellishment you made to bolster your reputation," David said.

"I may have embellished the Ritz story, but I... Look! It's underlined: **had one of the great parties of the war.**"

David picked up the picture of the two soldiers and the Leaning Tower that Hemingway had placed to the left of the computer. He turned it over and handed it to Papa.

"Dad & Friend," Hemingway read...

"How did you know the first word was Dad?" David asked. "There's only a capital D. It could be the man's name was David."

"The Iceberg theory of mine at work," Hemingway said. "A writer can leave out most of what he knows and if the writing is true, so true that the reader knows it is real, then the reader will understand."

"Dad & Friend," Hemingway read again: "Army...From France and Italy..."

Hemingway turned the picture and studied it again then stood it up against the stack of diskettes on the table to the left of the computer.

"Read pages 340 and 341, Papa," David said.

"You've got it memorized; too, have you like the pictures on the ViewSonic?" Hemingway asked, pointing at the computer screen, his forefinger beneath the word: ViewSonic...

"Yes," David said. "It's about you and the other reporters covering the war..."

"I see," Hemingway said reading. "Did you mark this?"

"No," David said.

"Tomas did," Hemingway said.

"I don't think so..."

"So you're thinking again..."

"Maybe," David admitted.

"So tell me who did it..."

"He did," David said, pointing at the picture. "The devilish one..."

Hemingway picked up the picture. Studied it again then leaned it against the speaker so it tilted backward and to the right.

"Martha Gellhorn, your wife is mentioned as doing an outstanding job, like the others there, but it says the best known of all was you then the next line says something about you being a jerk. What is that?"

"What the hell does..." Hemingway turned to the front cover: "this writer, Ambrose, know, anyway? His name is not listed is it?" he continued, opening the book as he spoke.

"Look on the next page," David said. "There are some underlined words about how you sat down to write and how your work was about what you saw, did, felt and how you carried vital information to headquarters and had many adventures and how there was much drinking and how the city was the one you loved best in all the world. I like it all. Not just what the man there in the picture liked. If that's what a jerk is, I want you to make me a jerk just like you."

"What's the other book?" Hemingway asked.

"It's about Ernie Pyle," David said, taking the paperback from Hemingway, hoping he had not seen the comment about Pyle seeing the war differently, especially the writer's remark that the difference was why Pyle was read fifty years later and Papa wasn't.

"He was a great reporter," Hemingway said. "His story about Captain Waskow is excellent prose. You need to read it, study it..."

David took the books to the balcony and placed them on the shelves where Tomas kept them.

"I know why we are here!" Hemingway exclaimed as David came into the bedroom.

"Why?" David asked...

"I met that man in Paris. I went to a bawdy house with MP's when they raided it. The man and his buddy both were in it. They crawled out across the rafters somehow and got out on the roof. When they dropped to the ground, they landed next to me. They thought I was an MP. When I convinced them I wasn't, we drank the rest of the night. I read Chapter Two of *A Farewell to Arms* to them. It was a hoot!"

"I'll read it again," David said. "I'll get it now and start."

"You can read it later," Hemingway said. "I want to finish my story. Those two men were truckers—part of the Red Ball Express that left Paris in late August of 1944 following in the wake of the German routs. It looked like the war would be over soon. Those truckers, few of them white like those two, drove twenty hours a day, driving deuce-and-a-half trucks bumper to bumper without lights at night. Even doing that, it was impossible for them to get fuel, food, and ammunition to the front lines."

Hemingway paused. David stood patiently.

"The next morning, early, the devilish one—I called him Cat the other Cat Man—went outside. They saw the humor in it—them coming out of a cathouse onto the roof and jumping down like alley cats. They could drink too. Anyway, next morning Cat goes outside and comes back in grinning ear to ear. I think I asked him if he'd swallowed the love birds in the hallway."

"He said: *I've got this dud* and he held up a bullet *and I'm gonna shoot it off the jerry tank of that jeep in the street* then he rushed out of the room again. Cat Man and I followed him."

"I started to tell him I wanted to shoot it, but I saw that the jerry tank was on the MPs jeep, the one that raided the whorehouse the night before and Cat Man snickered beside me when he saw that jeep. Now Cat waltzed over to the jeep and stood that bullet up on the jerry tank, the five-gallon gas can, and ran back to us. He had a Luger in his hand that he said he took off a dead German officer. He winked at Cat Man and drew down on that bullet. I figured he meant to hit the jerry tank and then I got mad at him because he pulled an Annie Oakley right there in front of me..."

"You mean he hit it like you hit the squirrel?"

"He did...set me up and that's what made me so mad. I couldn't much more than see it. My father could shoot better than I could and I doubted him...most, I imagine, I knew I couldn't have made that shot. I was ready for him, my right hand balled up and fixing to deck him when he started rubbing it in."

"What happened, Papa?" David asked when Hemingway paused.

"I asked him how he learned to shoot like that and he said: *when men come charging to kill you, you have to make every shot count. I've got a dud grenade here for you. I'll put in on the jerry tank and you can shoot it off. I know you can...*"

"Did you, Papa?"

"Cat ran across the street again and I didn't notice Cat Man leave, but when Cat started to put that grenade on the jerry tank, he turned to me and said: *come visit me in Kentucky and we'll go possum huntin'.* I liked him right then. I'd bragged about Africa to them. I killed big game for them with my words and talked about beautiful black girls. I got over being mad at him. I knew I could hit that dud grenade. When he put the grenade on the jerry tank, he ran like hell toward the left and I saw Cat Man slapping his right leg, laughing his fool head off. I leveled down, caught the thing in the front sight of my .45, and squeezed the trigger. The gun roared and the grenade exploded before the bullet got out of the barrel. The gas in the jerry tank ignited and lifted the back of the jeep, flipped it like a girl doing a somersault, and the streets filled with American GIs thinking the Germans had returned. I ran inside and cussed. That was the last time I saw either one of them."

"Now that's funny," David said.

"I didn't see any humor in it at the time. Look at this..."

David took the picture from Hemingway's right hand.

"Who is that woman?" David asked when he had seen the second picture.

"I don't... It's Catherine," Hemingway lied.

"It is not Catherine," David said. "Her hair is long..."

"Don't you remember how you liked her hair that way?"

"In the book you wrote that I did," David said, "but she is not one of your wives."

"Look at this," Hemingway said, holding the picture in his left hand and placing the index finger of his right hand across the woman's body where the strapless, blue dress began beneath her breasts. The finger emphasized the young woman's cleavage."

"She is naked now," David said. "Her right arm pulls that man's face down toward her upturned lips..."

"That man is a sculpture, a work of art chipped from the marble arch. The picture was taken in a church somewhere in Europe. My thinking is that it is in Germany, southern Germany, Munich perhaps."

"When you give me life," David said, "I want to be an artist. I want to paint and create sculptures."

"A writer is an artist," Hemingway said.

"Then I want to be two artists," David said. "Is that God's head, Papa?"

"Why do you ask, David?"

"If it is God, I will recognize him when I meet him."

"It is not God," Hemingway said. "Man can not see God's face and live."

"Can man look on an artist's face and live?"

"Yes, David..."

"You made her look like art," David said.

"No, David," Hemingway said. "I just wanted to make you look at her in a different way. I see in her what you seek. She is alive, witty and beautiful."

"I wish her hand was pulling my face down toward hers..."

"Now... Now..." Hemingway laughed. "You just set yourself up to be doomed—to be the man who falls as we always have."

Chapter Forty-one

Tomas had emailed the woman, asking several questions, but one he hoped she would answer in depth. He had asked: **What is it like to be a woman in today's society?** His plan was to start a new chapter with the question and her responses.

She did not answer during her lunch break as he hoped she would. As Tomas drove from work, he thought about the novel. In his mind, scenes began to form. His inner eye sorted memory, doing many things. At first the eye was hard, critical of his past, his relationships, and the two failed marriages. The eye softened, flashed images of two women he had helped, protecting one from a man who would have killed them to keep secret a crime he had committed. The next image was that of a woman with a lifestyle radically different from norms acceptable within a rural, agricultural community.

When the eyes in that community began to watch him, they became tongues, critics who read his actions, rewrote them, and advanced a new plot for each woman. He could not defend himself where the first woman was concerned without putting her at risk. Years later, he spoke honestly about the second woman, but no one except the woman knew the truth. He had been defined by those tongues, and the shape they gave to the story of his life, the negatives like corrections written in the margins of a manuscript, became the official, edited version.

As he turned into his drive, his inner eye became the frightened eye of a child when the image of a third woman, a beast that roamed within him as she always did, shifted his sight from the villain and heroes within to the world without.

Instead of asking her what it means to be a woman he thought as he walked from the garage to the A-frame *perhaps I should have asked myself what it means to be a man. Better still I should have asked her why she hides her words in the attic of her unconscious mind or puts them on the page, never letting anyone read them—reclusive, private with them as Emily Dickinson was.*

His hope was to tempt her to write, for she had expressed that desire. What he had learned on his journey through life could not be a benchmark for her. He wanted her to take her own journey. He saw his questions as an attempt to get her to see her own uniqueness. He did not know how she viewed them.

All that is profane or profound lies within he thought *and the universal begins there.*

Emily's words came back to him: *like to visit it, but I wouldn't want to live there.*

"I understand," he said, remembering the words: *all that is profane or profound...* words left on the note in the book for him to ponder. *I have never lived outside myself,* he realized.

His hope was that the woman would readily respond, but when she did not, he began to think she might be too private to make public her awareness of the feelings she valued, feared, or protected. He thought *she does not want anyone to know those things that make her who she is.*

As he went upstairs, he remembered reading that a woman, from the time men began to tell tales, stood for everything that could be known. Instead of writing his thoughts as prose, he captured his feelings. He wrote a poem.

Chapter Forty-two

"A poem?" David asked when he entered the loft. "Did you write it?"

"No, David," Hemingway answered. "If I had written it, you would have already seen the words. Tomas wrote it."

"What's it about, Papa?"

"It's about a woman," Hemingway said, "and Tomas. It's a poem about one moment in his life."

"What kind of moment?"

"The kind you want," Hemingway said. "One where one part of you comes out and celebrates life while the other part stays put, observes, reflects, and writes. Maybe it describes the separation Plato tried to explain..."

"Can it be so simple?" David asked, thinking: *Why don't you let me read the lines myself?*

"Read it!" Hemingway said. "I'd almost forgotten how he called his work lines. He did not want to be called a poet."

He's reading my mind again David thought, asking: "Tomas?"

"No," Hemingway muttered. "Crane..."

"I like the ending, Papa. You were right. That is how I want to be. Who was Crane?"

"The man who wrote *The Red Badge of Courage...*"

"I remember reading how that book influenced you," David said. "Did Tomas write like Crane?"

"No, Tomas wrote this poem like Estlin Cummings wrote his poetry, words running together or suddenly breaking apart, falling down the page or across inside ungrammatical, punctuated clues."

"Did you know this Cummings?"

"He was studying art in Paris when Hadley and I were there."

"Part of the Lost Generation?"

"Damn, you're like a sponge. What you read gets soaked up by that emptiness where your brain should be. He experimented with language and form like Eliot, Pound, Stein and Passos did."

"But you chose not to experiment..."

"Dreisler, Anderson, Robinson, and Frost chose the same path that I chose. Just as

Cézanne was a contemporary of the impressionists, so were we. As an artist, he went beyond impressionism with its individual brushstroke and the fall of light onto objects, to create, in his words, something more solid and durable, like the art of the museums. As writers, we, the lost ones, created words that endure."

"I want to read all those writers," David said.

"Look," Hemingway pointed at the computer screen, "his sketch of Elaine. She was his first wife."

"Without her arms," David said, "she'd look like a giraffe…"

"Bravo… Bravo!" Hemingway clapped. "That is how a poet sees."

"You made me a writer," David said. "I want to learn how to write—write well."

"Estlin was an ambulance driver in the war…"

"Like you were," David said, "and Tomas' father."

"Why do you say that?" Hemingway asked.

David went to the landing and returned with two books of poetry.

"I wrote poetry," Hemingway said.

"I remember, Papa," David said. "From the time you were twelve... Wrote from the time you were alive..." he added, smiling. "Some critics said you were as brilliant and troubled a poet, as you were a novelist and human being. They considered your early poetry to be a good indication of what you were soon to create."

"The many that were written to individuals," Hemingway complained, "were not meant to be published."

"I'd not be surprised if your poems are good... I've read the one in Tomas' book about the war," he said, "but none of his in this one with the woman on the cover. There's a poem he wrote about his father getting blown out of a foxhole in Italy, near the German border. He wrote they made an ambulance driver out of him after that. I'm going to read the one with the woman on it, but you should read it first."

"Why, David?"

"You've had lovers you can imagine going back to..."

"And those I should have run from..."

"And you will know if the book is real, Papa."

"I only know that a woman can't change the width of her hips or the faults of her parents," Hemingway said.

"Why did you say that?" David asked.

"Many children get abused before they are nine," Hemingway said. "By a neighbor next door or..."

"You by the bitch in your own house!"

"Not the same abuse, David, but you've got the picture."

How will I be able to write about a woman, Papa?"

"I don't know if I can help you with that. Don't you remember you asked me why I wrote such lousy women?"

"I shouldn't have asked that..."

"I could tell you anything, David, but you have to meet a woman. When she is new to you—the first time you see her, take it all in: the length of her hair and the smell of the shampoo she uses, the sound of her voice, and recreate her in words so a reader sees her face, smells her hair, and hears her voice. On the other hand, David, Mark Twain wrote that women are almost always incomprehensible by any rational standard."

"What does that mean?"

"It means a man can only portray the women in his own life, the way he sees them— the way he treats them or they treat him. If he can't do that, he ends up writing his fantasy of them. I don't know, David. I wrote true sentences about hunting, fishing, and prizefighting. I wrote with directness and vigor; with the accuracy of a man who handled the artifacts of those sports, took them apart, and loved them. But women..."

"I will learn to write them."

"Good luck," Hemingway laughed. "I spent my life with them, with women who could not come enough or who could come too easily. A man who ends up with either kind cannot write about the experience. The best he can do is fail; some critic will write that he's only presenting male fantasies..."

"I read where you beat up your wives," David said, ducking Hemingway's left arm.

"Let me tell you something, David!" Hemingway roared, "I never did that sober. Sometimes a man has to get drunk to deal with things. Getting hit over the head with a hangover gives a man or a woman temporary amnesia."

"I read..."

"Damn it! If it's about me, don't quote it!"

"I was just going to say I read that a man has a woman inside him and a woman has a man inside her. How can that be?"

"It's confusing, David. The brain is made up of two parts, one for thinking and one for feeling. The cognitive side rules over what someone called masculine traits. The feeling side rules what someone else labeled feminine traits."

"Which side is which?"

"Right side is feeling—left side thinking," Hemingway said. "Then the rule of opposites applies..."

"What does that mean?"

"You can read about that on your own..."

"When I'm alive?"

"If you're ever alive!"

Chapter Forty-three

"Have you finished reading them?" David asked when Hemingway appeared holding the two books.

"I swear," Hemingway, said, "he wrote this one for you."

"Why do you say that?"

"Just listen," Hemingway said, reading:

Inside the woman,

**he became a poet
able to take
wild words
from their darkness
into the light
of the page.**

"He's writing about a woman," David said.

"Yes, he is. That's only the first stanza. I wanted to see if you remembered. After reading his book, I feel like I know Jack's Knob and Old Seventy Creek. He paints them well with his words."

"While you were reading, I finished everything he's brought home with him. I found the book, *Poems of Stephen Crane*, in the bookcase. The editor wrote that Crane's method was like that of a painter. I heard you say Cézanne began painting the way impressionists of his day did, using light and dark to convey feelings. Must a writer write details like some artist painted?"

"Slow down if you want me to answer," Hemingway said. "I mimicked Cézanne. He was one of the great forerunners of modern painting. He put down on canvas exactly what his eye saw in nature. That fit my style. Neither Cézanne nor I received encouragement from our families. Cézanne's parents felt he had little talent, his strict father insisted that Paul continue in law school even though he wanted to begin painting full time. My father was strict. He ruled what I could read in our house, but he let the Bitch rule him! I learned to understand Cézanne much better and to see truly how he made landscapes when I was hungry for words like you are, David. Estlin had that same hunger. He rebelled against his preacher father—spent the man's money on booze and women. As for Crane, another preacher's son, the realization that he could write poetry came when he was struggling to earn a living as a journalist. Writing words on a page like an artist paints a canvas fit Crane's style of writing. When you start your own work, make every sentence, every word important."

Do I have to study art to write well?"

"Even Picasso wrote poetry…"

"Who was Picasso?" David asked.

"An artist I met in Paris. He picked up where Cézanne left off. His work is abstract, and modern, cubist, looks the way Estlin wrote his poetry."

"I will study his art and read his poetry," David said.

"If it takes studying art for you to learn to write, then study art, or study music. A writer prods the reader with magnified visual detail and repetition. Those become the coloring necessary to complete the different portions of a verbal canvas. Journalism can be a launch pad for creative writing. Read and read before you start you own writing. Start with a complete thought and go on from there. Don't stop until you've got a poem, a short story, or a play…"

"Did you draw or paint?" David asked.

"In high school my drawings for science were good. Some artists can draw the human form at rest, in dance, and in any shape the mind can conceive. I loved the class. It helped me focus on the world of nature I treasured so much. I wrote my name on the pages of that three- ring binder notebook, and made detailed sketches of animals we dissected. I may have written my first true sentence following an experiment we did. I recounted the classroom examination of specimens, and I drew a smelt in fine detail."

Your mother made you..."

"Don't mention that bitch again!" Hemingway bellowed. "Don't mention my father! If you forget and ask me about either, I will write your suicide upon those eyelids of yours!"

Chapter Forty-four

Tomas wrote an email to the woman: *I sure hope I have not offended you in some way. That was never my intention. The book is progressing. I would love to read some poetry. Send me some email when you can.*

He read an email from Emily: *hey, Tomas~ well, I finally started on your book. It's very intriguing so far! It's a quick, easy read, which means the writing must either come swiftly to you, or it's been a difficult story to put together. I'm going to guess it's the first, knowing you (the little bit that I do know you).*

Let me finish more (I should finish it by this weekend) and then let's have lunch to talk about it?

Ps. I just started on chapter nine and I thought, wait a minute! That's me! I'm honored and flattered and humbled.

Your friend, **em**

It was Monday. Tomas processed bills and documentation for travel expenses, reconciling the travel advance and actual expenditures, for Jill in accounting, and worked up timesheets and student stipend lists for Nicole in payroll. He dropped the paperwork off on his way to lunch.

When he entered Cranmer Dining Center, he heard a familiar voice call out: "I've finished reading the book, finally. Come join us. Let's talk about it…"

He looked to his left. Emily waved and Nate smiled. He went through the cafeteria line and took his tray of food to the table where Emily and Nate were.

"So how was David Bourne?" Tomas asked as he joined them.

"It was great so far," Emily said. "Look at you, Tomas, eating so healthy."

"I work out at the fitness center with Nate," Tomas said. "I try."

"I'm in the book," Nate said. "I read it."

"Everybody who talks to Tomas ends up in the book," Emily said.

"Not everyone," Tomas said. "Only the ones who say something…"

"I didn't know the meaning of David's names until I read what you wrote or made up for the story."

"That's the way Hemingway wrote and a risk a writer takes with autobiographical writing. Hemingway wrote about food, drinks, showers, swimming, riding bicycles, and always looked at words as though he were seeing them for the first time," Tomas said.

"I remember the drinks," Emily said, "even how to mix them. I'll have to go back and read about the other things now. I've tried to read *Out of Africa*, but I can't get into it. "

"Maybe it's time for you to start writing," Tomas said.

"All you have to do is write one true sentence," Nate said.

"I'm impressed!" Tomas said.

"I am, too," Emily said.

"It's what you have taped to your desk," Nate said. "I just repeated it."

"My favorite quote," Emily said. "My favorite author..."

"Do you want to take me to Cleveland, Nate, so I can drive home the car I bought?" Tomas asked.

"I don't think so," Nate said.

"I think I'm going to get my sister to drive me to the airport after work today. The woman who sold it to me left a message on my cell saying snow would start there this week, Thursday's the prediction. Lake effect snows there can pile up a foot or more in a few hours. If I don't get it before the snows start, I may have to leave it there all winter," Tomas explained.

"I'm interested in the woman you're writing about," Emily said. "Your woman friend... I'm anxious to read more about her."

"She may not be in it anymore," Tomas said. "I've got two different versions in mind— one where she returns, wanting to be a writer— one where she stays in the background, a spring that feeds the well that I am writing from..."

"She has to come back," Emily said. "She's my second favorite part. My favorite is still Hemingway doing his about face and saluting the picture of the soldier on the wall."

"I'll get you more to read soon," Tomas said. "Did Nate tell you I was going to change the date for bringing our students to campus? We're going to bring them here on your wedding date so we can crash it just like in the movie. Have you seen *The Wedding Crashers?*"

"We saw it together," Emily said.

"That'll be us," Tomas laughed.

"Oh, no!" Emily exclaimed.

"Thanks for letting me join you for lunch," Tomas said, thinking he would leave them.

"They've got carrot cake with whipped cream icing for dessert," Emily said. "I'm going to get a piece and you're going to share it with me."

"Don't tempt me," Tomas said. "I'd have to do more sit-ups than the one hundred twenty-five I did yesterday."

"Without stopping?"

"Without stopping," Tomas said.

Chapter Forty-five

When Tomas got back to his office, he had an email from the woman: *You've not offended me at all; I have been incredibly busy. I apologize for putting you off. I'll try to get back with you on answers to your questions some time this evening. I'll be in touch.*

When she did not get back with him, he emailed her the following morning: *I'm going to leave an envelope with the novel I bought for you and a diskette of the one I'm writing where I have left books before. You can pick them up* Tomas emailed the woman. *Please let me know whether the book I'm writing is going to stand on its own.*

Chapter Forty-six

When Tomas stopped at his sister's house, she told him she had a migraine. He did not ask her to drive him to the airport in Nashville. Instead, he decided to drive to Lexington and ride a bus to Cleveland. Betty, the woman who sold him the Corvette, had called earlier in the day to tell him that tomorrow, Wednesday, would likely be the last day of good weather in Northeast Ohio. Lake effect snow was Thursday's prediction.

"Once the snows start here," she said, "they pile up. Don't worry though. We'll keep the car in the garage until you can get here. It won't matter how long that takes."

He wanted to park the car in his own garage. As he drove, he told himself *this is a risk worth taking.*

He stopped in Somerset and ate at *Back Yard Hamburgers.* He drove from Somerset to Nicholasville and called Terry, his son.

"I'll meet you at the house," Terry said. "I've been unpacking boxes at the apartment tonight. The trucks have been out already, putting chloride on the roads. We're on the dividing line between heavy snow and an ice storm."

Terry drove him to the Greyhound Bus terminal before ten PM.

"I'll be out in a few minutes to let you know if I can get a ticket," Tomas said as he opened the passenger door to get out.

"Take your time," Terry said. "I'm in no hurry."

Tomas waited in line for fifteen minutes while two attendants argued with three young men. From the exchanges, he understood that the men had missed their bus and were making demands that the women could not honor.

"May I help you?" one of the women finally asked.

"Elyria, Ohio," he said. "One-way..."

"That'll be sixty-nine dollars," the woman said.

Tomas handed her four bills and she gave him back two, a ten and a one. He went outside to tell Terry he would see him tomorrow. He went back inside and waited. When the bus arrived, it was more than an hour late. He waited outside the bus while a woman, her three children, and a man who had volunteered to watch over them boarded.

As he stood on the second step, the man asked the woman on the front window seat to move her carry-on bag so he could sit.

"I'm handicapped," she said. "I won't."

"Yes you will," a man in the second row said, standing so she could see his Greyhound uniform."

"That's not what they told me when I bought my ticket!" she shouted.

"This bus will be full," the man said. "Every seat will be taken. Move you bag!"

"I told them," the man said to Tomas, pointing toward the woman and her children, "that I would look after them."

"I heard you in the terminal," Tomas said. "I thought that was honorable of you. Take your time."

The woman took time to put on her shoes, but she did not move her bag from the aisle seat. The Greyhound employee reached over the seat and placed the bag in the woman's lap."

"Put it under your seat," he said. "The man's has been nice to you."

The man sat. The man in the second row sat, and the woman wrapped her arms around the bag as though she were protecting valuables.

"Is anyone sitting with you?" Tomas asked the woman in an aisle seat three rows behind the driver's glass protected cubicle.

"Yes," she said, pointing toward the carry-on bag in the window seat.

"Is anyone sitting with you?" he asked an elderly gentleman in an aisle seat seven rows behind the driver. He had helped the man with a vending machine earlier inside the terminal waiting area.

"No," he said.

"Every seat will be full!" the driver shouted as he entered the aisle. "Make room. We've got to get moving now."

"Here's a seat, young lady," Tomas called to the black haired young woman in the aisle who began to move toward him, followed by a second young woman, a blond.

"Young man," the woman who had told him the window seat was taken stood, putting her carry-on bag in the floor," your seat is ready."

Tomas moved toward the woman while the blonde made her way toward the rear of the

197

bus. She turned and followed Tomas toward the front.

"Anyone with you?" he asked the man across the aisle from where he and the woman would sit.

"No," the man said, flatly.

"Here's a seat," Tomas said to the blond.

"Thank you," she said as the man moved from the aisle seat to the window seat so she would not have to climb over him or past him if he stood.

When Tomas sat in the aisle seat, the bus driver turned off the overhead lights and pulled out of the parking lot. The stench in the seat where the woman's bag had been was almost unbearable. He could tell the woman was aware of the scent. He was glad she did not talk to him. He did not want to know what was in her bag.

It was twelve fifty AM when the Greyhound bus pulled into the Cincinnati terminal parking lot.

As they prepared to disembark, the driver said: "Everyone has to get off the bus. The crew will be servicing and cleaning the vehicle. We'll be here about fifteen minutes. I'll give you a reboarding pass so you will know to get back on when you hear them call out number 486."

Fifty-five minutes later, the call went out for all passengers with number 486 reboarding passes to begin loading at gate 3. Tomas got on the bus near the front of the line, choosing a window seat two rows behind the driver. A young lady entered the bus, looking toward the back seats.

"You may sit with me if you like," Tomas said, hoping she would choose to do so.

She did not.

"That lady is moving back," she said. "I'll sit behind you. I like a window seat."

Behind the young lady, a man Tomas took to be Mennonite looked toward the rear of the bus and removed a large hat, the kind a country music star of rodeo bronco rider would be proud to wear.

"Is anyone sitting here?" he asked Tomas as he put a suitcase in the luggage compartment.

"No," Tomas said, wishing he could lie because a stench only somewhat less putrid than the woman's carry-on bag preceded the full-bearded gentleman.

While the other passengers boarded, the man leaned back in his seat and closed his eyes. Six other Mennonites boarded, moving toward seats scattered from the mid-section to the rear of the coach. When the driver, a woman who had replaced the previous driver, honked the horn and began to back from the parking space, Tomas leaned forward, resting his head on the back of the seat in front of his. The driver turned off the interior lights and maneuvered the bus from the lot, snowflakes hitting the windshield and melting. Another female driver sat in the front window seat where the woman who said she was handicapped had ridden. Tomas smiled, remembering how the handicapped woman had walked gingerly around the terminal waiting area. She changed buses in Cincinnati, bound for Detroit.

"No smoking, drinking alcohol, or loud music will be tolerated on this bus", the driver announced. **"If you have young children, please accompany them to the restroom at the rear of the bus. Go in with them. Young children like to lock the door, but they never know how to unlock it. There's no key until we get to Columbus. That's a long time to be locked in a bathroom."**

Near Georgetown several minutes later, the man beside him leaned forward, and Tomas moved backward, resting his head against the back of his seat and the window, cold against his left brow. The Greyhound employees talked incessantly from Cincinnati to Columbus.

At three-forty AM, the driver parked the Greyhound in parking space number four. An attendant came from the terminal and motioned for her to back out of the space and park in number five.

"Now what the hell's the purpose of that?" she asked.

"I don't know," the other driver-passenger answered.

"There's not another bus coming in to take this space. He should know that," she said, honking the horn then shifting the bus into reverse.

The driver did not cut the steering wheel to the left as she backed the bus. She ended up trying to park with the right side of the coach over the left line in parking space four. She hit the wooden barrier that shielded the metal uprights posts.

"Nobody heard that!" the driver shouted, honking the horn to back out again.

No one spoke up.

"If he don't like it," she said, parking again, "I'll tell him I saw a mouse. I'm afraid of them. I can't help myself."

"I don't blame you," the other Greyhound employee chimed. "Scare me too, they do!"

The driver laughed into the microphone as she announced: **"You may stay on the bus if you like. We'll only be here a few minutes. If you must get off, take a reboarding pass. Those of you making another connection need to give your baggage claim ticket to the man out there. He'll get your luggage."**

The Mennonite stood, put on his coat and hat, and took his suitcase from the luggage compartment. Tomas looked back toward the rear of the bus. The other Mennonites put on their coats and took their luggage from the overhead compartments. Only three other passengers got off.

Tomas napped until he heard the thud of a suitcase into the upper storage area above him. He opened his eyes. The Mennonite smiled, removing his too large, black hat, and his coat.

"I thought this was Mansfield," he said.

"No, it's Columbus," Tomas said. "This bus doesn't go to Mansfield."

"In there, they told the driver to take us and two other passengers to Mansfield," the man said, sitting and leaning back.

Tomas leaned forward as the other passengers boarded.

The driver and her friend boarded last. The driver turned out the interior lights and honked the horn. They began to talk, the driver and the other woman. Tomas listened to them, but he did not actually hear their words until the bus had traveled some distance beyond Columbus.

He heard the driver ask, "Do you remember Nancy's daughter?"

"Yeah," the other woman answered.

"They offered her sixty thousand to work in the kitchen..."

Tomas thought the driver was referring to Greyhound Lines, Inc., the company offering, but...

"Is she going?" the other woman asked.

"I don't think so," the driver said. "You know, they offered me a hundred thousand to drive a bus. I considered doing it for a couple of days. I guess thinking about how in Iraq a bus driver never knows when a terrorist might climb aboard wearing a bomb made me choose not to go. You've seen what happens when they do that."

"I wouldn't have considered it for a moment," the other woman said. "Just think—a driver would never know when some kook might open fire on a bus load of people, hoping to kill Americans, even an American bus driving woman would make no difference. No, not me..."

"I'd send my boyfriend though," the bus driver said. "He's seventy. All I'd want is an insurance policy with my name as the beneficiary."

"My boyfriend's eighty," the other woman said. "I'd send him, too."

The women laughed and joked as though they were the only two people on the bus. Tomas napped, waking to a silence that puzzled him. He looked out the window to his left. The two lanes of the road opposite the Greyhound bus were white. He looked ahead—the road glistened. The road was not I-71 north. He figured it was an eastbound highway, one with hills.

The driver pumped the brake pedal repeatedly.

Why doesn't she gear down? Tomas asked himself, imagining the bus going into a skid.

The driver pumped the pedal and Tomas felt the bus pick up speed as the right rear wheels locked.

"Let off the brake!" Tomas shouted. "Gear down!"

"You a trucker?" the driver asked.

"Trucks, big tractors, you name it," Tomas said, talking about farm trucks loaded with hay or tobacco and large Ford tractors.

"Thanks for reminding me," the driver said. "We get down this hill and we're home free."

At the bottom of the hill, the driver and her friend began to talk again.

"You know what?" her friend asked.

"No," the driver said, "what?"

"They make me mad again," the woman said, "and I'll fall down the steps."

The driver laughed, saying: "Your luck you wouldn't break anything—just get bruised."

"Wouldn't matter," her friend laughed. "I'd go to the hospital with my back killing me. They can't tell when you're faking a back injury cause nerves don't show up like a broke bone."

The bus terminal in Mansfield was dark. A white van, parked near the highway, was the only vehicle in the parking lot. The driver stopped on the right side of the white building and opened the door.

"Watch your step as you get off," she called from outside.

The Mennonite and his traveling companions got up; put on their coats, got their luggage from the upper luggage racks and when the man who sat with him put on his black hat Tomas leaned back.

"*Sei sicher,*" Tomas said in German.

The man looked at him, smiled and answered, "*Sie auch...*"

The man took his time going down the steps. The second Mennonite, a young man in his twenties, rushed past Tomas then started down the steps. Tomas heard his suitcase hit the bus as he slipped on the ice and fell backward.

The other Mennonites and two young ladies got off the bus without falling and the driver got on. As she drove away, Tomas saw the Mennonites loading their luggage in the white van. He felt sorry for the two young ladies, however, for they stood with their backs toward the east wall of the terminal, breaking the prevailing wind, but providing no warmth in near frigid conditions. He hoped they would not have to wait there long before family came to get them.

Tomas could see pink sky toward the east as they entered Cleveland. When he looked toward his left, he saw Jacob's Field, home of the Cleveland Indians. To his surprise, the driver exited, drove straight for a short distance, turned right for a shorter distance, then right again and stopped at a red light near the entrance to the stadium.

"Where are we?" the young lady in the seat behind him asked.

"In Cleveland," Tomas said.

"Did we stop in Columbus?" she asked.

"Yes, we did," Tomas said. "Did you miss your connection?"

"I think I did," she said.

When he stepped off the bus at the terminal in Cleveland, the driver asked, "do you have any luggage?"

"Just me," he said. "That's all there is."

She smiled and said, "Enjoy your stay."

Inside, Tomas saw at once that Cleveland's terminal was a more traveler friendly facility than any of the others he had seen during his trip. Signage, displayed above the doors, gave the destinations of each departing bus. He saw two gates with Elyria above the doors. He went to the line with Chicago as the final destination and Elyria as the first stop and stood for a few minutes. He saw the young lady who sat behind him and slept, missing her connection. She stood at the ticket counter, crying.

Tomas stepped out of line and went to her.

"Problems?" he asked.

"I wish I had accepted your offer in Cincinnati," she said.

"You had no way of knowing that I wanted you to sit with me because I thought you would smell good."

"No," she smiled. "I really judged you wrong."

"You thought I was hitting on you," he said.

"I'm sorry," she said.

"Don't be," he said. "I could have been the kind of man your mother warned you about..."

"No," she said. "I spent four days and three nights with him. I'm supposed to get married tomorrow at three o'clock."

"And you can't get there from here," he said.

"I've spent too much of my money," she said. "I called the man..."

"The one your mother warned you about?" Tomas asked when she paused.

"Him," she smiled, easing the frown lines on her forehead. "He got what he wanted. He wouldn't help me. I can't call home and ask my father to use his credit card. I'm not supposed to be here. I called my girlfriend. She tried to use her card, but it's full."

"How much do you need?" Tomas asked.

"I have some money left, but not enough. What I need for the plane fare is less than eighty dollars, plus taxi fare of thirteen to fifteen, the lady at the ticket counter said. I had her call. Should I call my boyfriend and confess?"

"Do you want to call off the wedding?" Tomas asked.

"No," she said. "I know now that I want to marry him tomorrow. I did not realize that five days ago. Cold feet, I guess..."

"Here," Tomas said.

The young woman looked at him, at the bill in his right hand.

"I can't," she said, starting to reach toward him.

"Take it," he said.

"I will send it back to you," she said, taking the money from his hand.

"I've got a connection of my own I have to make," he said. "Be happy..."

"I think I will," she said. "What is your name?"

"I'm nobody," he answered as he rushed toward the second gate with Toledo as the final destination and Elyria as the first stop.

He was tenth in line when the gate opened and a woman stepped inside.

"I'm ready to load all those passengers who were given reboarding passes," she said.

Tomas did not have one. He waited until twenty passengers loaded. He looked behind him. The line was long. He looked to his right. A young woman stood beside him. She took her ticket from its envelope and smiled a wicked, mischievous smile.

"Are you going to Toledo?" she asked.

"Only to Elyria," he said. "Are you just beginning your travels?"

"No," she said. "I've been riding all the way from New York. I'm going home to Toledo. I hate New York."

Tomas was not immune to her looks. He heard a voice in the back of his mind saying: *You are as beautiful as a May fly.*

He looked around to see if it was really a voice in his head. He saw a man looking at them but the man turned away quickly.

"You look great," he said to the woman.

She blushed.

A woman who can't blush is worthless Tomas heard the same voice calling from deep inside his head or, he wondered *is it my voice,* because his voice was not the one he heard...

Then the voice, unmistakably not his, said *the pain of a woman who breaks hearts all around until she falls, briefly...*

He looked for the man, but the man was gone.

"New York is too big," the young woman said.

Tomas opened the door and held it while the attendant took the woman's ticket and then took his.

211

"Thank you," the woman said. "They don't have manners like that in New York City. You sure you aren't going to Toledo?"

"Only to Elyria," he assured her. "I'm picking up a car I bought and taking it home to Kentucky."

"What kind of car?" she asked.

"A Corvette," he said, noticing her slender neck, how immensely attractive, coy and alluring she was when she smiled again, and *dangerous* he thought.

The Woman, pausing for a moment as though in quiet reflection, suddenly turned her feet toward him.

Where the feet go, the heart follows he heard the voice again and looked over his right shoulder. The man was there again, but not as close this time.

"Move along, you two," the attendant said.

The young woman leaned toward his ear and whispered, "I'm not the person you see. I'm a good woman..."

"You couldn't sell yourself, could you?" Tomas whispered.

"To a million men with one glance," she said, kissing him lightly on the cheek, "but not to one on a New York street."

"Move along you two!" the attendant shouted. "This ain't a place for you to have sex. This is a place for buses and passengers."

The young woman ignored the comment; smiled at Tomas and said, "a good woman makes history in a man's heart."

Her words rang so true that Tomas regretted having thought of her as dangerous, but the voice returned with a caution that made Tomas smile. The voice said: *Trout are lured by artificial flies more successfully than with real worms.*

The young woman hurried to the bus. When Tomas got up the steps, he looked for her. She sat in a window seat near the back of the bus, talking excitedly to another young woman who sat in the aisle seat to her left. She looked up, saw him, and smiled. At a distance she gave off the same air of feminine sexuality that he saw when she cut line to get to him.

Tomas sat in the window seat two rows behind the driver, a different woman.

I never had to look for a subject to write or a woman to love the voice in his head said *both sought me.* He turned around and saw a man's left arm close the bathroom door. There were no empty seats. He shook his head left to right, telling himself it could not be, then nodded three times. When he looked at the young woman, she shook her head left to right then nodded three times...

The driver honked, backed the bus, and drove from the parking lot.

"There's no smoking of cigarettes, pot, or crack cocaine allowed on this bus," the driver announced. **"If you do smoke, tempt a friend to puff with you for when I throw you off. That way you won't have to stand out there in the cold all by yourself."**

Forty minutes later, at eight-thirty, Tomas was the only passenger to get off the bus at the Elyria terminal.

"Are you Tomas?" the woman in a maroon van asked as he started toward the building.

"Yes," he answered.

"I'm Betty," she said. "The one with the Corvette... Get in!"

Tomas walked around the front of the van and got in.

"Wish I hadn't parked here. We're blocked until the bus moves," she complained. "I hope you don't mind cigarette smoke."

"I don't mind," Tomas said, thinking *it's your vehicle and I'm not that rude.* He looked up, and waved at the young woman whose face was pressed against the glass as the bus moved forward.

"We'd best go get a thirty day tag," Betty said, "so you can get out of here before the storm hits."

Chapter Forty-seven

"Come look at this new picture he put on the computer," David shouted.

"What kind?" Hemingway asked, having appeared behind the desk chair.

"A woman," David said. "She looks like Hadley, but I don't think it is. She's not your type..."

Hemingway waited until the pictures changed, one after the other.

"It's not Hadley. It's Louise Brooks. You're right and you're wrong. She's not my type in that pose. It's her feminine side." Hemingway said.

"But it's her left side," David said. "You said left side was masculine—right was feminine."

"Photographers understand the rule of opposites I told you about..."

"I remember," David said. "You said I'd have to read about that on my own if I ever am alive."

"Well, you're not going to have to, now, David. The rule of opposites is simple to see in a picture. The left hemisphere of the brain controls the cognitive functions attributed to the male make up of an individual. The right brain controls feelings, intuition, attributes labeled feminine. "

"That's..."

"Don't interrupt me!" Hemingway exclaimed. "Photographers learned, and taught each other, how to pose men and women to highlight masculine and feminine looks. The left hemisphere controls the right side of the body— the right controls the left side. If I was a photographer and I wanted to make a model— male or female—look softer, more feminine, I'd shoot the left side. If I wanted to highlight the harsher, rugged masculine look, I'd photograph the right side."

"I get it, Papa," David said.

"So now you don't have to read about the rule of opposites," Hemingway smiled.

"Who was she? One of your women?" David asked.

"She was the symbol of an era," Hemingway said. "A dancer, an actress, a bisexual woman..."

"Like Marita and Catherine," David said.

"Yes, just like I wrote them," Hemingway said.

"What does bisexual mean?"

"To make love to a man or a woman without feeling any guilt or shame…"

"Woman making love to another woman I know from the book. Do men make love to men?"

"Yes, David," Hemingway said. "Some do."

"I'm glad you didn't make me that way," David said.

"I didn't make you homophobic," Hemingway laughed. "You've become that on your own or Tomas' women made you that."

"Did you mean for the novel's bisexual theme to be a stark departure from your masculine themes? Could I say the story reflects tenderness and vulnerability that you normally hid behind your public image?"

"Is that what you read?"

"I don't believe I did…"

"Original thought," Hemingway said. "A bit long winded, but undoubtedly your first…"

"Her hair is short..."

"Not a man's, exactly," Hemingway explained. "Her mother took her to a barber and got her braids cut off—a Dutch bob with a fringe down to her eyebrows. I remember reading that she was about ten years old and had just begun to dance in public. What parents do to their children often can not be undone..."

"Like what your mother did to you when she dressed you like a girl and let your hair grow in locks," David said. "That was just the opposite of what her mother did."

Hemingway reached behind the computer and picked up the notebook and a pencil.

"That was not a question!" David yelled. "That was a comment the same as you made..."

"You're pressing your luck," Hemingway warned, putting the notebook and pencil behind the computer. "You keep trying to get me to talk about the bitch and my father. Well, here's all you're ever going to get out of me. Father was..."

"Dr. Clarence Edmonds Hemingway, a large bearded physician more devoted to hunting and fishing than to his practice," David said, smiling.

"That's not what I was going to say!"

"Sorry, Papa," David said. "Go on..."

"You go on! Tell me whatever else you've got to say about him now! Then I'll say what I have to say!"

"He had the lures that snagged you out of troubled water. He gave you a fishing rod when you were three and a shotgun when you were ten."

"Is that it? All you've got to say?"

"Yes, Papa," David said.

"He was a big man on the outside, but in so much pain inside, so passive, a coward stuck in a marriage that was wrong. He hunted and fished in order to save his masculine soul. The bitch..." Hemingway began.

"Grace," David said, "a religious-minded woman who sang in the choir of the First Congregational Church. She gave you a cello, and made you practice on it for a year."

"Hell! Shut the fuck up! I was going to say the bitch dominated him, wanted me to be feminine, a twin to my older sister Marcelline. If you don't think that's a crock of shit, you don't know anything..."

"It was!" David exclaimed. "I read how it..."

"Fucked me up? Made me question my gender? If it was true, it was true. If it wasn't, it was real..."

"The part of the iceberg we can't see?" David asked.

Hemingway looked at David. After a moment, he smiled.

"That fashion," Hemingway said, pointing at Lisa Brooks' profile when it appeared, "was called a *Buster Brown haircut*. Buster Brown was a cartoon character, a young boy whose mother dressed him up like a sissy—damn you! Don't you say just like my mother did!"

"May I think it?" David asked.

"Damned good grammar, David," Hemingway smiled. "Buster was no sissy. Far from it, he was all boy, an incorrigible one, in fact. The bob was a cut designed to look girlish on a boy and boyish on a girl. It was a mark of unsettling androgyny rather than being just a child's cut."

"What does it mean?"

"Androgyny?" Hemingway asked.

"Yes, androgyny," David said.

"*Andr-* or *andro-* from Latin and Greek means man or male," Hemingway explained...

"She made you study Latin and German," David stated.

Hemingway glared at David, but was silent.

"Not a question," David said. "I was talking to myself... What does it mean?"

"*Gyne* means woman or female," Hemingway said." The word itself means being both male and female. One of the two creation accounts in Genesis you read provides evidence for the androgyny of God, the Creator: So God created man in his own image . . . male and female created he them."

"That's the way it was," David said. "You said it almost word for word!"

"Almost!"

"Exactly!" David beamed.

"Don't play semantics with me, son," Hemingway warned.

"No, Papa," David smiled.

"In their innocence in that first garden," Hemingway said, "Adam and Eve knew nothing of sex or gender. It was as though they were fused together in perfect and harmonious unity..."

"Plato," David said, "back to back..."

"Don't interrupt me!" Hemingway shouted. "Fused in an archetypal androgyny until the serpent—until their fall into sin... Knowledge opened their eyes to sexual difference, but also gave them a consciousness of their own incompleteness."

"The forbidden fruit," David voiced his understanding.

"And do you know what that fruit was?" Hemingway asked.

"An apple," David said.

"It was the sweet taste of a woman's sex," Hemingway said.

"No! It was an apple," David argued. "I know you know it was..."

"Because you read it?" Hemingway asked.

"In your novel *A Farewell to Arms,*" David smiled proudly. "You wrote that it was the apple of reason."

"You have to remember," Hemingway said. "I was young then..."

"How young?"

"Older than you…"

"How old am I?" David asked.

"Depends," Hemingway answered.

"Upon?"

"Whether you count from the time they published *The Garden of Eden* or your age in the novel itself?"

"In the novel…" David said. "The age you made me…"

"That would be your early twenties," Hemingway explained. "Not nineteen…"

"The preferred age of draft boards and recruiters," David said, remembering their earlier conversation.

"You do have my memory!" Hemingway explained.

"Therefore," David smiled again, "the fruit was an apple."

"Have it your way," Hemingway laughed. "But one day read what Mark Twain wrote in his work, *Extracts from Adam's Diary.*"

"What did he write?" David begged.

"He wrote that the forbidden fruit was not an apple, it was a chestnut..."

"It wasn't. It was an apple..."

"He didn't see you," Hemingway said.

"God?"

"Tomas didn't see you at all," Hemingway said.

"You mean on his trip? When you followed him?"

"Yes," Hemingway said. "When you were following me..."

"Is that bad?"

"It could be good," Hemingway said. "Maybe we weren't following him. Maybe I'm in control..."

Chapter Forty-eight

Tomas had not seen the Corvette, except pictures of it that Betty had sent. She drove to the license bureau and walked into the long office where she took the number fifty from a dispenser on a load-bearing post near the counter where three women worked. ***Now serving number forty-two*** flashed in red letters behind the women.

"Is that the right number?" Betty asked. "We're the only ones here?"

"No," a woman said. "We forget to change it. Number forty-eight... (No one came forward.) Number forty-nine... (No one answered the woman's call.) Number forty-nine..."

Betty went to the counter. Tomas followed.

"We want a thirty day tag, Joann," Betty said.

"That'll be ten dollars fifty cents," the woman said. "I'll need to see your license and social security card."

Tomas gave her his card and Kentucky driver's license.

"We can't do this," Joann said.

"Why not?" Betty asked.

"Your husband has to sign it in front of a notary... The lady at the end of the hall can handle that for you."

"What if he calls in from work?" Betty asked. "He's on a point system. One more point off and he loses his job. At the beginning of January, his points start over..."

"He'll have to come in here if you want the tag today," Joann answered.

"I'll call him," Betty said. "Maybe his boss will let him work over to make up the time. That way he won't lose his job."

Tomas went to the first of four rows of folding chairs and sat in the second chair from the left. Betty made the call and sat next to Tomas in the first chair.

"Here," Tomas said, handing Betty two bills. "I'll have my banker wire the rest as soon as we get to your house."

"Rick said to make sure I got the money before he would sign for the notary, but I said you would not cheat us."

"You were right," Tomas said.

"They all know me here," Betty said. "They tried to indict me for homicidal manslaughter when I wrecked and the airbag killed my two-year-old granddaughter. I see Ricky coming in now. I'm going to tell him we're giving you the car. That will save you seven hundred dollars."

Betty rushed to meet him when he entered the room. They talked for a minute or less then walked toward Tomas.

"Glad to meet you, Ricky," Tomas said, standing to shake the man's hand. "I hope this didn't cause you any problems at work."

"I've been there so long," Ricky said, "they let me do what I want."

The woman at the end of the hall motioned for them to come to her desk.

"You need to sign above your name," she said. "I'll notarize it and you can get the thirty day tag. How much did you get for it?"

"We're giving it to him," Ricky said, signing.

The woman notarized Ricky's signature and gave him the certificate of title.

"Here you are," Ricky said. "I'll get back to work. If you have any questions about the security system, just give me a call."

"I will," Tomas said, leaving Ricky and Betty.

"I'll have the tag ready for you in a few minutes," Joann said.

Tomas went back to the second seat from the left in the front row of chairs. Betty continued to talk with the woman at the end of the hall. He looked back at Joann. She motioned for him to come to her window.

"That'll be ten-fifty," she said.

Tomas paid her.

"Thank you," she said. "Have a safe trip home."

"Thank you," Tomas said. "You have a great day."

"I only live a couple of miles from here," Betty said, walking toward the door.

Tomas followed her, shivering as he walked to her vehicle. She got in. He got in and looked at the tag. It was valid until January 5. Betty backed from the parking space and drove slowly toward the traffic light, speeding up when it changed from red to green.

"See," she said as she drove up a hill with a deep ravine on her left," we do have hills here. You should feel right at home."

Tomas did not answer, thinking: *this is no steeper than my driveway. She should drive up Coal Bank Mountain.*

"Here's where I hit the break in the road and my wheels went like this," she said, throwing her right and left arms out, indicating that both tie rods had broken. "I hit that wall. It killed my little girl."

"I can't imagine how that would be," Tomas said.

"I had a premonition that someone hit me in the back—I do that all the time... think about something bad and it happens. Except this time I saw the wreck, but I didn't see it like it actually happened. It was the only time I ever put her in the front seat. I think about her—see her every day and night. It's..." she stopped speaking.

"Like a soldier flashing back to a firefight, I imagine," Tomas said.

"I hope you are hungry," she said.

"I ate at every stop we made," Tomas said. "I'll just take off as soon as we get the money wired in to your account."

"I told my husband—well, he's not actually my husband any more. I divorced him. I told him to put gas in the car for you, but he didn't. This station on the right... You can drive up here and fill up. I only live at the end of the street there," she said pointing right as she turned.

"That'll be okay," Tomas said.

"Did you figure out how to get back to Kentucky?" Betty asked, turning left and a quick right into her driveway.

"If you'll let me use your computer, I'll see if I can't take the Ohio Turnpike to Interstate 71. If so, I know how to get on home from there."

"From the gas station I showed you," Betty said as she opened the car door," turn right and go to the first stoplight. Turn left there and you can pick up the Turnpike on your right about a mile down the road."

"Sounds easy enough," Tomas said, getting out of the car.

He followed Betty into her house. She introduced him to the babysitter.

"This is Dee Dee," she said. "Dee Dee this is Tomas."

"Pleased to meet you," Tomas said.

The woman nodded as she put the child, a boy, into a high chair near the table and across from the chair where she sat when they entered the kitchen.

"Where is your computer?" Tomas asked.

"I forgot," Betty said. "It's in here."

Tomas followed her from the kitchen to the small room on the right. He waited until Betty established an Internet connection then sat in front of the monitor. Betty returned to the kitchen. Tomas looked at the address on the certificate of title and typed it into the mapping program. In a few seconds, the route appeared. It was as he had thought it would be.

"Any luck yet?" Betty called from the kitchen.

"Yes," Tomas said. "I can get there from here. I take the Turnpike to Cleveland and pick up Interstate 71 to Cincinnati. When I cross over the Ohio River on 75 South, I'll be in Kentucky."

"How long will it take you to get home?" Betty asked.

"Ten hours," Tomas said, walking toward the kitchen.

"You go in there and wash up," Betty pointed toward the bathroom. "Breakfast is ready. I don't want to hear a word about you taking out of here until you've eaten."

Tomas did not protest.

"Want some coffee?"

"No," Tomas said. "I don't drink it."

"Tea?"

"No," Tomas said.

"What is it you drink—milk and water?" she asked.

"Mostly water," Tomas said, returning to the kitchen, "but I also drink milk."

"Sit there," Betty pointed toward the end of the table. "That's my seat. Nobody sits there but me."

Tomas nodded at the baby in the high chair. It smiled at him.

"My son's child," Betty said, pouring milk into a tall glass. "I bought this for my daughter. When she gets drunk in a bar she can find her beer."

Tomas chuckled as she sat the glass in front of his plate. A rainbow of colored lights illuminated the rim.

"You can turn that off," she said.

"How?" he asked.

"I'll do it," she said, picking up the glass, tilting it and flipping a lever.

"My daughter," she began her story, "met an eighteen year old when she was fourteen. He got her pregnant. She had my granddaughter when she was fifteen. The granddaughter I told you about. Her boyfriend got killed in a car wreck right after she was born. She met another man. He got her pregnant. He overdosed and died. Then she met another dope head...He killed himself. She was pregnant again. She smokes, takes pill—all kind of dope and drinks. Her second child was a boy. He stayed with me until I wrecked. She took him after that. He still cries for me, but she won't let me have him. I could take her to court and get him, but I don't want to have to do that. Her third child was a girl—born black from the waist up, but they saved her... I saved her. I used to be a nurse before I messed up my back in that wreck. I'm on full disability now. I told her to let them take the baby and she told them she wanted them to and the baby is alive today. She's with a millionaire now. I introduced her to him, but I didn't know he was a dope head, too. I'm going to have to break them up."

"Thanks for breakfast... I wish you luck with your daughter," Tomas said. "I'll call the bank now and have the money wired to your account."

Chapter Forty-nine

Tomas followed Betty outside. He opened the door of the Corvette and looked inside. The seats were not as new looking as they had appeared in the photos. He taped the thirty-day tag onto the rear window. He got in and adjusted the steering wheel. He turned the key, but the engine did not spin. He knew it would not start.

It's a good thing I didn't offer the woman a ride to Toledo Tomas thought.

"We'll jump it off," Betty said, going to her van.

Tomas got out of the Corvette and pulled the back of the driver's seat forward. He opened the cover of the battery compartment and removed a black plastic cover from the negative post and the red plastic cover from the positive post.

"Ricky must have taken the jumper cables to work with him," Betty said as she came back to the Corvette. "I can't find them anywhere. I'll go call him. If he has them, it won't take us long to drive over there and pick them up."

Even though the battery would not turn the starter fast enough to start the cold engine,

Tomas did not regret his purchase. The car and the beautiful woman gave him the same feeling that came each time he wrote well. He wondered if the woman in Kentucky felt that way about her words. He wished she would bring some of her writing, written in that way so he could help her better understand and know the value of taking nothing but words and creating nothing less than literature.

"He had them in the house," Betty said, carrying the booster cables toward the Corvette.

Tomas took the cables and said, "Betty, you'll have to turn and back up on this side of the car."

"You mean the battery's behind the seat. I never would have found it. I would have looked under the hood. I might as well tell you about the car," she began. "When Ricky and I got married, he did not drink. Then he started drinking to get drunk. I told him if he would stop drinking, I'd buy him anything he wanted. He wanted a boat. I bought the one he liked. He stayed on the Lake every minute he could that summer and fall. When winter came, he started drinking again. I sold the boat. He drank to get drunk all winter. When spring came, I told him I'd buy him anything he wanted if he'd stop drinking. He wanted a Harley. I bought him the kind he wanted. He rode it all spring and summer. When winter came, he started drinking and I sold it. I divorced him. He came back two years later, wanting me to take him again. I told him if he would not drink, I'd buy him whatever he chose. He wanted a Corvette. I told him if he started drinking, I'd sell it. He drove it less than one hundred fifty miles and started drinking. He hit something with it. You saw that small hole in the front... Well, I'm selling it to you. If he doesn't stop drinking, I'm kicking him out."

Tomas hooked the red cable to the positive post of the van's battery and the black cable to the negative post. He stepped from the van to the Corvette and clipped the red cable to the Corvette battery's positive post and clipped the black cable to the negative post. He pushed the seat upright and sat in the driver's seat. He turned the key, the starter whirled the engine quickly and the engine started, turning too many rpm's until the choke disengaged. He got out of the car. Removed the cables from the Corvette battery and the van's battery and gave the cables to Betty. He closed the hood of the van and put the black and red plastic covers on the Corvette battery's post. He got in the car, rolled down the window, and waved at Betty.

"I'll be off now," Tomas said as he began to ease the Corvette backward.

"Call me if you have any trouble," Betty said. "He never drove it on a long trip. It's been stored for years now."

"I'll let you know when I get home," Tomas said. "Thanks for breakfast and good luck with Ricky and your daughter.

Chapter Fifty

"Who was Hunter Thompson?" David asked Hemingway.

"I don't know," he answered. "If I ever knew, I don't remember. Why do you ask?"

"I read where he killed himself because you were his hero--how he wanted to die like you did..."

Hemingway did not reach for the notebook and a pen or pencil. Instead, he paused for a long time.

"I guess it's time to cover that ground with you, David," he said. "I understand why people want to die, but I never wanted to be a nexus for death."

"But you were," David said. "After you killed yourself, your sister Ursula committed suicide and your brother, Leicester. Adriana Ivancich, whom you loved and the woman you used to model Renata in *Across the River and Into the Trees*, also killed herself."

"Oh, hell no!" Hemingway cried out. "In Latin **Renata** means reborn. She gave me new life. How could she? I never ran into her out there or anyone I ever knew..."

"It is true. Your son, Gregory... And your granddaughter..."

"No! Say it is not so!"

"I read it in Tomas' papers," David said.

"You wonder how I could fall prey to the terror of living, and therefore kill myself. Death was never a metaphor for anything else. When I offered death as an alternative in my work, I meant death. My father killed himself. Hadley was the child of a suicidal father. When I was leaving her for Pauline Pfeiffer I thought to remove the sin out of her life and avoid Hadley the necessity of divorce . . . by killing myself. But I said the only real reason for not committing suicide is because you always know how swell life gets again after the hell is over. I knew as well as I knew the sun would rise that the hell would never be over for me. That's when the call to die, the final call, came. It came to me a million fold."

"I do not want it to come to me," David said. "I must write..."

"Words live in a stream, in a downward rush, in a drop, in a fall, in a current and in an undercurrent. Like the trout, a writer must maintain balance in both of these powerful currents and reel in the hungriest of the lot of those words to build a sentence," Hemingway said. "If you would write like me, you must write so as to contain the tension, as a nervous laugh contains a terrible cry, for that was the heart of my method."

"I would that you had never created me if you can never set me free," David said.

"My friends said I grew away from everything before I died. Gary Cooper's death was hard for me to take. Cancer dried him up. He was nothing of the man John Wayne and I hung out with, killing lions. With those two, I wanted to be a part of everything, and of course I really was..."

"I want to have friends like they were, Papa," David said.

"You should have seen Coop... No, David, you have to see him in the movie, *A Farewell To Arms...*"

"I want to see it. Tell me how it was?"

"It was a Hollywood Classic. I would have none of it at first, but I met Coop. They did the best they could with it. Coop made me proud and Helen Hayes... She was the right one to play Catherine. She looked like I wanted my girls to look. It was a World War I love story. I can't tell you how many times I watched it, but I can say I still love that nurse..."

"I will write you back to her, Papa. Give me life and I will get up early. I will always write in the morning. Then there will be another swim or a fishing trip..."

"You only know how I did it. It may not be that way for you. On Sundays, I always wished to go to a bullring or to the cockfights. If you ever see a cockfight, will you recall every peck in the tease or each time a metal spur pierces a lung? I could."

"I don't have those experiences yet," David said.

"When you go..."

"When?" David asked in disbelief.

"I said when you go, David," Hemingway said. "Watch everyone—study them, but most of all watch the cocks and their handlers. Feel the excitement—capture it—capture the smells, the smoke in the air, and the sweating man beside you then write those smells in you mind. Learn what it means to compete, David. Watch the winners and the losers! When handlers tease the cocks, paint the raised hackles..."

"Hackles?" David asked.

"**Hackle**, David, a word with many meanings. Learn them all. On the spinning wheel downstairs there is a hackle, a board with teeth for dressing flax, hemp, or jute, but hackles on a gamecock are the long feathers on the neck, the saddle of the bird. In the tease before two birds begin to peck each other, watch how those hackles rise up like an erection, David. Paint a picture of them with your words, David. Write the truest thing you can about them. Let the reader get the rush a soldier gets on the battlefield. Watch the experienced handler blow into his gamecock's beak before he tosses it into the ring. Life's a journey, David. Life's a battle. Live it, love it, and leave it like a man when it is time."

"I want to tell stories like you can, Papa," David lamented. "I have to!"

"The would be lover, who works so hard to attract another, and the writer, who works for the affection of the reader are one. They employ the same behavior. They travel to the center of their own journeys. My work remains, my art functions, and the critics who praised themselves for calling me unworthy came around to saying that the unworthy one's fiction worked on the soul of a reader who was not insensible to it. You keep asking me to do the impossible, David. You might be better off to ask me if it is possible for a man to commit suicide a second time. What you ask me is nothing less than fantasy and imagination, story and image, but you cloud each of those because you want me to explain my death. I will tell you only what is true. There is much you will not know about it, but do not ask. Is that clear?"

"Yes..."

In the end I, and not Mary or my doctor, knew what I would do. I told him how much better I was. But I knew I would never be better again for I could not write, neither write from my heart nor from my head. When I could not write in my head anymore, it was the worst. But it was more complicated than that," Hemingway paused.

David did not ask anything—did not speak at all.

"The strange thing was how I heard screaming in my head every day and night. I don't know who was in there screaming. I don't know how many there were in it. We were at home. I could do nothing to stop the screaming, David," Hemingway paused again.

David nodded.

"When morning came, it was a false morning. The screaming was the problem. Where to be happiest... I needed to write. I could not write those screams. If you become a writer, do not be impressed because you have written a beginning, middle, and an ending. Write to keep the screaming out of your head, not keeping the screaming out, but existing with those screams in there until you hear your own voice louder than all the screamers. Only then will you hear, not the other voices, but the one true voice of everything, and you must make that voice your work. You must train that voice to fight, to raise its hackles against the other screamers, and protect it, David. Above all other things protect your voice!"

"I will," David said.

"And help your readers..."

"How?"

"Help them to understand the relief they feel when they realize that their own lives do not encounter such dangers. Then they will know your work is profound."

"I need to encounter some danger," David said.

"I'll see that you do, son. One generation passeth away, and another generation cometh: but the earth abideth for ever, David," Papa quoted. "From the Bible... Ecclesiastes 1:4...the next verse after that gave me the title for my novel, *The Sun also Rises*. You don't know those things yet. We have a lot of ground to cover, David...you and I... One day, these things should be the greater part of you. At this moment, they mean nothing. It was Descartes who pointed out, consciousness is the only thing that surely exists; yet, here we are..."

Chapter Fifty-one

The cell phone rang. Tomas turned the turn indicator lever to the right. Tired, having driven but an hour, he turned into the first rest area on Interstate 71 south of Cleveland.

"Hello," Tomas answered the caller.

"This is Betty, the one you bought the Corvette from," the woman said. "How's it going?"

"The car's running better every mile I drive it, Betty" Tomas said, thinking: *it would have made it to Toledo.*

"I was just worried," Betty said. "I got to thinking how bad I'd feel if it were to break down on you."

"It will make it to Kentucky, Betty," David said.

"You just got out of here in time," she said. "Snow is falling fast... We could get five inches or more."

"I've been hearing that on the radio," Tomas said, "but I'm running ahead of it. I've only seen a few flurries."

"Well, call me when you get home," Betty said.

"I will," Tomas promised, getting out of the Corvette and walking to the vending machines inside the nearest, glass-enclosed structure.

It was less than an hour later that Betty called him while he pumped gasoline at An Exxon station.

"I know you're going to think I'm acting like your mother," she said, "but I want to know the car is as good as I think it is. We've already got more than five inches of snow and could get a foot more."

"I'll call you when I get home," Tomas said.

She called him twice, however, before he got home. Each time she asked him how the car was doing and told him about the snow that kept coming in off Lake Erie. As he turned into his driveway four hours later, he dialed her number.

"Mom! I'm home," he told her and she laughed.

Chapter Fifty-two

At Cranmer Dining Center the next day, Nate and Curt joined Tomas for lunch.

"Let's hear it," Curt said, putting his food on the table and his tray on the floor.

"You mean the story?" Tomas asked.

"What's happened now?" Curt asked.

When Nate came to the table, Tomas told them the story of his bus ride and the two women in the Cleveland terminal.

"She had the exotic appeal that draws men in like flies. She had that one -look allure that sets everything in motion. I don't know how to describe it except to say it is so much more intense than the attractions of women who want to make an emotional commitment."

"So you went to Toledo?" Curt asked.

"I know she wanted me to say I would drive her home," Tomas said, "and I was tempted, but I kept saying to myself that I couldn't. What if I had started to Toledo with her in nine-degree weather, in a car I knew nothing about, the wind chill hovering near zero, and the car just quit on the interstate. What would I have done?"

"When you got the car," Curt asked, "what did it do?"

"It wouldn't start," Tomas said.

"Then you made the right choice," Curt said. "You meet the most interesting people of anyone I know."

"It's all a lie," Tomas teased. "I just made it up."

Nate laughed, and then turned to Curt and said, "I told you he was a big fish," as he got up and returned to the cafeteria.

"I think I'll get some fruit," Curt said, following Nate.

"I didn't eat much," Tomas said. "I think I'll have some dessert."

When Tomas returned with a slice of pecan pie and a scoop of maple nut ice cream, he looked at Curt's bowl.

"Is the fruit cherry or strawberry?" Tomas asked.

"It's low-fat," Curt said of his ice cream.

Tomas sat down and began to eat.

"You know," Curt said, looking over Tomas' shoulder, "I don't like frail women. I want my women to be at least five pounds over weight."

"I'm sure we can find you one," Tomas said as Nate joined them. "I'll start looking for one right now."

As he got up to leave the dining center, Tomas wished he could write words that could capture readers like the woman had captivated him.

He saw a familiar figure exiting ahead of him and heard the voice in his head say *write words so strong that no matter how many times they've read it or how they feel about the manners and morals of the characters, they won't be able to resist its spell.*

Chapter Fifty-three

Hemingway turned on the computer and clicked on Tomas' novel. He scrolled to the last page that Tomas had written. He looked at the page that was white, empty except for the chapter and number, written in sixteen-point font and bold type.

Hemingway typed: ***you are a traveler at heart. There will be many journeys.***

"Are you writing that for me?" David asked as he ran upstairs.

"For Tomas," Hemingway said, "and for me."

"Even words that are not meant for me," David said, "I can see. I am you, Papa. I want to be me."

"When I wrote you into the novel, I actually heard my father's booming voice in my head saying how filthy my words were and how you characters were disgusting. That made me as happy as the Nazis made me when they burned my books in their bonfires in 1933. I was seeking and experimenting when I created you..."

"Some critics thought you had lost your footing, your direction..."

"Pound was the only critic I ever trusted," Hemingway said. "He took me under his wing and let me incubate. When I came out, I knew not to trust adjectives and I knew how to compress my words into images. I worked slowly and told everybody how hard it was to write."

"I can't write anything," David complained as he had done before...

"You are me, David, at the end when I tried so hard to write something for President Kennedy and I couldn't write that one true sentence. I admired the man. I could not step up to the plate without striking out. I could not score a touchdown. My myths had died. You were right, David, when you said I was a liar."

"You did not lie to me about the bull, Papa" David apologized. "That was you dressed in white in front of the beast."

"The beast was harmless. Its horns were soft like my penis..."

"The man on the ground might not agree with you," David said. "It was after you. Its head was down and you were in front of it. I could see how horny it was."

"It had horns, David," Hemingway laughed, "but they were tipped with rubber."

"I remember," David said. "It was the woman who was horny..."

"Look!" Hemingway pointed at the computer screen when it darkened and the picture of a bull kudu appeared. "I think I will write you inside a woman with long corkscrew horns like those..."

"I don't want a horny woman!" David shouted.

"You will change your mind, David," Hemingway laughed.

"I won't," David said.

"You want what you have never touched. I will make you horny, too, David. In my work you will be horny. I will write you into a modern tragedy, son, one in which you will have to solve the puzzle that is unsolvable. You will thank me for writing you that way. You will make the noble sacrifice that we all admired in lovers. You will not throw away what could be true love just because the woman you are with is horny and the sex takes some work, you'll see."

"You don't have horns. Your women did not have horns. I don't want horns!"

"What you really want to become is a whole person, David," Hemingway said. "Don't you?"

"Yes," David said.

"You don't want to have to give up all of life's usual intimacies, and all of its associated connections for which you so yearn, do you?"

"No," David answered.

"Maybe I was wrong when I said the words I wrote were for me and Tomas only. You have not yet journeyed into adult human sexual arenas. You must be horny to do that. What you don't understand is the fact that horny is only an emotion..."

"Emotion?" David asked.

"A longing for the so-called other whose presence will allow you to quit searching. He didn't see you again," Hemingway said.

"I know. I stood next to him," David agreed. "Nobody sees me..."

"Unfortunately, I do," Hemingway said.

"I heard you talking to him..."

Hemingway laughed.

"You should have seen that Cuban ground's keeper run the first time I went back to Finca Vigia, my home from 1939 to 1960. It was on the darkest of nights when he was leaving the estate. I whispered in his ear: *Do you need a built-in, shockproof, shit detector?*"

Chapter Fifty-four

When Tomas checked his messages on the last Friday before Christmas, one was from the woman. He opened it first and began to read:

Better late than never.

It has probably been 6 weeks since I last wrote a poem.

My mood is usually desperate when I write poetry, and it is very evident.

I'm a one-track person, there is no way that I could listen to music and write at the same time... But if I were going to, it would definitely be blues.

Lost love is almost always my theme or possibly the unfairness of the world.

I'm a real "get-you-downer".

No, I don't drink wine, but if I did it would be red; it just seems more romantic that way. I drink mostly Crown, tequila, and domestic beer. Very simple, I am.

I don't read very much poetry and all that I remember from college was Robert Frost; but that's a bit common to repeat.

I personally think that it is wonderful to be a woman in today's society.

Women have earned an ounce of respect; just enough to make it in the working world if they're built that way. But have earned just little enough that men are still expected to be "responsible" for women. That's not a bad thing. I enjoy going to work, but even more I enjoy a man leading the way, opening the door and paying for dinner. It's the best of both worlds in my opinion.

My favorite things about life, hmm...new love, close family, the smell of fresh cut grass, solving a puzzle, discovering that you're capable of something, men in suspenders and ties, fast cars, high heel stilettos, motorcycles, the song Amazing Grace, deserved cigarettes, tight jeans and sweat and every single thing that causes it. There are a lot more but I figure that will do it.

Most like to be said about me: That there is much more to me than it appears. That you have to know me to understand me...

Most hate to be said about me: That I'm as shallow as they first thought.

Of course the Corvette is red and tan.

I'll send you a poem later.

He read the email again before he sent her a brief reply: *I am glad I came to work today. I am on my way to Lexington. Now I have material to work with, and quite revealing it is, too. Have a Merry Christmas and drop by if you find time. I have something I want to give you. Hope to see you when I see you.*

The second message he opened was from a New York literary agency that had requested a query and sample of his poetry. His heart began to pound as he read:

Greeting and Congratulations!

255

Our agency is prepared to offer you a contract for acceptance as our client for agency representation based on:

1) The poetry you submitted...

Tomas did not read the rest of the message. He printed the contract and took it to the Kia. He would have the weekend to read it and fill in the blanks then sign it.

Chapter Fifty-five

"I'm glad you came up," David said as Hemingway entered the loft bedroom. "Sit."

Hemingway sat down as David moved away.

"I want to show you the neatest thing," David said. "I watched Tomas do it."

"What is it?" Hemingway asked.

"Something that would have made writing easier for you..." David began. "Type these words: **a story by any other name, that affected an equality of purpose,** and this word: **fricking.**

"Is that last word German?" Hemingway asked. "When I wrote *A Farewell to Arms,* the editor made me use an underlined blank space for that forbidden term..."

"Just write the words on separate lines," David pleaded.

Hemingway typed:

a story by any other name
That affected an equality of purpose
frikking...

"Look!" Hemingway pointed at the green underlines and the red one.

"That's what I wanted you to see," David said. "If you go back up now like this and push down the left button on this thing, like this in front of *a* then go up here where it shows <u>T</u>ools like this and push down the left button again, read what you see on top."

"Spelling and grammar," Hemingway read.

"Now push down on that..."

Hemingway did.

"Read it aloud," David said.

"Capitalize the first word of a sentence," Hemingway read.

"Now go back up and push down the left button in front of *an* and *equality, too.*"

Hemingway did, fascinated.

"Now do what we did before," David instructed.

"Like this?" Hemingway asked, completing the task without hesitation.

"Exactly," David said. "Now read..."

"It gives the rule for number agreement: If you are using a noun that cannot be counted or divided such as..." Hemingway silently read the rest of the rule.

"How about that?" David asked.

"Useful," was Hemingway's only comment.

"Now go back up and push down the button on the red underlined word," David said.

Hemingway did and clicked on <u>T</u>ools, then on <u>S</u>pelling and Grammar, reading without being told: "Not in dictionary... The word: frikking is in red letters, not underlined in red like it was. The thing has a dictionary!"

"Yes, it does," David agreed, "how many suggestions does it give for the word?"

"Six," Hemingway answered, "but not the word: **fucking,**" he said, closing the window by clicking *Cancel,* then typing again the word: frikking.

"Your writing was your work," David said, "but look how this takes a lot of the work out of it."

"I used to add up the numbers of my words in the margins. My spelling was an atrocity. I had the ability to accurately recall the smallest of detail in a scene or in dialog. I could capture odors, tactile description, the temperature, the glint of sunlight on a trout stream, but I had trouble with spelling."

"With this," David said, "you can go back up and click on the red underlined word and push down on Backspace here and the word disappears or you can choose one of the suggested words from <u>S</u>pelling and Grammar in <u>T</u>ools and your spelling problem is no longer a problem. Try it..."

"I'll just type it again," Hemingway said, typing: frikking and highlighting the word then hitting backspace. The word disappeared. He laughed then typed it again and chose the word: freaking from the list of suggestions.

"Type something," David said, closing his eyes.

Hemingway typed and David read each word aloud: **There is a certain ambivalence of death and violence. In the face of death, whether on the battlefield or in a drunken brawl, the human mind finds some good... Afterwards, if one survives the wounds, real ones that maim and scar, those scars, the maiming and the healed deformity inherent in them, bear witness that the past was real while the physiological wounds teach a priceless philosophy.**

"I'm out of breath," David said, opening his eyes.

"I love it!" Hemingway shouted.

"I do, too, Papa!" David shouted.

"I'd better backspace and get rid of all these words before Tomas gets home," Hemingway said, becoming serious again.

"I think there's an easier way," David said. "I've watched Tomas do it. He pushes the left button down from the right side of the page and moves up to the top of the page on the left then he pushes the backspace."

"Like this," Hemingway asks, following David's directions.

"Yes," David said, going into the bathroom and peering through the vertical blinds. "Hurry! He's home!"

"Hell's fire!" Hemingway cursed. "Damnation!"

"What's wrong?" David asked coming up behind Hemingway.

"I destroyed his work!"

"What?"

"It's all gone. I hit backspace and all that is left is the heading: **Chapter One**. I've done the worst thing anyone can do to a writer."

"Maybe not..."

"Are you going to quote me again or tell me what some critic wrote? Didn't you find where I said they made me sick?"

"You said they wouldn't even whore," David said, "whatever that meant..."

"Hell, son! It means what it means just like saying death is a whore meant what it meant!" Hemingway bellowed.

"Well, maybe..." David raised his voice, "my maybe, whatever it means, means what it means, too."

Hemingway, as though calmed by the words, looked at David.

"When your wife, Hadley, lost that suitcase of manuscripts..." David said, "You did not quit writing, and I am going to say what a critic wrote. He wrote that losing your work might have been good for you. Trying to remember the words, you wrote better. And I think he was right..."

"Why do you say that?"

"Because you knew it, too. Remember how you made me get out my pencils and sharpen them?"

"Five of them," Hemingway said, "and I wrote you as though you were able to overcome Catherine's burning of your manuscript, rising like the Phoenix from the fire, and finding the words came out of your mind almost intact."

"That's what I wanted you to see..."

"It wasn't that easy, David. Creativity is a struggle. It can push you to greater depths than you want to go. It can extract its price or it can demand payment: booze, drugs, even your sanity. You have to learn to walk on the edge of insanity without falling over that edge. Van Gogh is a perfect example of just such a walker..."

"Another artist?" David asked.

"Yes, David, you'll want to study him, and see the art that came out of him during his walks. T. S. Eliot, not an artist except for the fact I've mentioned to you that all writers are artists, said we have to arrive at where we started and see it clearly for the first time, David..."

"If it is real to him," David said, "he will sit down like you had me sit down and he will write his book again, for the words will not resist returning..."

"It is lost," Hemingway moaned and disappeared.

Chapter fifty-six

Tomas stood in the driveway outside the garage for a while, thinking about President and Mrs. Luckey's annual Christmas dinner. In particular, he recounted the conversation he had with Nate and Curt about writing.

"I'm going to write even though I've waited until I'm this old," Curt said. "I'll write a novel about old things, dinosaurs, wizards, and fantasy."

"Tell him how to write, Nate," Tomas said.

"Tomas is writing in his mind now," Nate began. "He's looking around and listening to everybody. He'd say, like Hemingway, that you have to write the truest thing you know."

"Then I'll write about what I'm drinking," Curt said. "What would Hemingway be drinking if he were here?"

"A *Papa Doble*," Tomas said.

"What's in it?" Curt asked.

"Two and a half jiggers of Bacardi White Label Rum, the juice of two limes and half a grapefruit, then six drops of maraschino and crushed ice. They tell a story in Cuba about Hemingway drinking sixteen of them, nearly sixty ounces of alcohol, and walking out on his own."

Curt cocked his head to the right and gave a look of disbelief as his answer.

"The man was a legend in his own time," Tomas said. "His journey through life was a mythical trip inside himself..."

Tomas went inside the A-frame and walked up the stairs to the loft bedroom. The computer was on. He went to the chair and sat down, reading: **Chapter One.** When he saw that there were no more words, he clicked on the red square at the top right hand corner of the screen. The computer program asked: Do you want to save the changes you made to "New Novel"? He clicked No. He turned off the computer and went downstairs, walked to the garage and carried in wood for the fire, washed his hands, and went to bed.

Chapter Fifty-seven

A medium sat at a round table where only one candle in the middle gave a feeble glow to the dark room. Surrounded by six college students, three young women and three young men, she had called forth Hemingway, unaware that David was not far behind.

"Give us a sign, Papa," she pleaded. "Speak through me from the Other Side, for these young people love you, they love your work, its style, and the way your writing cut away all of the frills. That's one of the things they want you to talk about..."

David appeared next to Hemingway. The two of them stood behind the medium, a woman dressed like a gypsy, though actually a hairdresser from Miami.

"You were male in your first earthly incarnation, Papa. Your profession was a designer, engineer or craftsman. In your past life, you were a seeker of truth and wisdom. You were born somewhere around Central Africa in 1675..."

"Africa," David whispered in Hemingway's ear.

"*For Whom the Bell Tolls* and *The Old Man and The Sea,*" the woman spoke, throwing her

266

head back, "stand out as two of my best... He's with us!" she shouted. Her voice deepened as she spoke and she pulled the arms of the female student on her left and the male student on her right toward her body.

"This is bullshit!" the female student shouted, jerking her arm free.

"You bitch!" the medium shouted. "He was here. You broke the spell. He was going to talk, but no! Just pay me my money, Sam..."

"It's Harry," the student to her right said, reaching for his wallet.

"She's a fraud!" the female student shouted. "We've been here an hour and I say that was not Papa speaking... She doesn't get a dime..."

"I like this girl," Hemingway said to David.

"Short haircut and tan," David commented. "She looks like a boy..."

Hemingway reached over the woman and snuffed out the candle.

The medium screamed when Hemingway pulled her ear.

"While we're this close," he laughed in the dark," we might as well go over to my house.

I want you to see my studio. It's on the second floor like Tomas' but outside the main house in a carriage house. The last time I was there..."

"That was funny!" David laughed. "You can be..."

"A handsome devil," Hemingway said, disappearing.

Chapter Fifty-eight

The New Year began with clouds against the western skyline in the morning, but by mid-afternoon the weather was as warm as Good Friday. Tomas took a box of flower bulbs from the basement and planted sixteen amaryllis bulbs between the daffodils that he had previously planted. The daffodils would bloom in early spring, but the amaryllis was a plant that would grow green blades in the spring, die down in late summer, and send up one central shaft to bloom in early August. Tomas called the amaryllis in bloom a naked lady. When he was young, a neighbor had called the flower by that name and it stuck with him through the years.

He walked from the flowerbed, along the driveway toward the highway. On the red bank opposite the stone pillar that held his mailbox, he planted lilies that would bloom in June.

He remembered the red berries in the pint jar in the gazebo and went there when he covered the last bulb. In the shaded area near the bluff, he dug between two large rocks that had been removed by a backhoe when the septic system was installed. He planted four of the thirteen Ginseng berries there and walked around the bluff and dug the remaining nine berries into the soil near a deteriorating sycamore log.

He thought about writing as he climbed from beneath the cliff, working his way up this time instead of going up and around as he had descended. He paused before he began to climb past the final overhang toward the gazebo and the deck on its north end. He wondered if his current work had become a story that just would not gel. He had other stories and folders of poetry in boxes that did not come together. Stories that didn't work... Poems that did not look like poetry... Stories that resisted illumination... Words that did not sound like poetry...

He had agonized and fantasized, but each story, each poem resisted its birth. He had completed one manuscript, a novel about a young man named Driver, but no matter how he tried to tweak it or tease it or curse it, the work kept going nowhere. When he finally realized the story was not worth pursuing, that Driver was not a character real enough to want life, he put the manuscript in a box that he took to Clement Shelley's boat storage where he had rented a space for almost seven years.

When Tomas climbed past the overhang and stood on the deck, he felt life coming on as though spring had arrived. He did not write that night. The next day, in the afternoon, hail the size of golf balls, covered the ground outside his office. A tornado moved past but so near that Tomas knew it was there. When the rapidly moving thunderstorm played out, the warmer temperatures returned.

Chapter Fifty-nine

When Hemingway sat in front of the computer waiting for the file to open, David joined him.

"I'm glad we went to Key West," David said.

"Are you suggesting that the detour gave you some insight?" Hemingway asked.

"I felt like you were there…"

"I was," Hemingway laughed, "with you."

"I don't mean that," David said. "The trophies on the walls, the penny in the concrete, and your old typewriter are what struck me most. I can see you standing up typing in the carriage house…"

"Only the dialog," Hemingway reminded him.

"Your prose was always done with a pencil," David said. "I remember."

"You should see my Cuban home," Hemingway said. "I'd like to take you out to my favorite fishing spot so I could see you pulled out of my boat by a marlin."

"I want to see it and Oak Hill and the Sawtooth Mountains in Ketchum..."

"Because my grave is there—not because of the splendid view?" Hemingway asked.

"No," David said.

"Yes," Hemingway said. "It's okay; I'd lost all confidence in the next life by the time I was looking out over those mountains."

"Maybe," David agreed.

"There's nothing in this world like Africa though, son, unless it is being young, but not too young to be taught something. I cannot teach you much anyway, but you have a good start as it is. Readers want to see the ugliness in a work, David. They sometimes say they don't. They don't want anybody thinking they know what evil is or how much of it they possess. They wouldn't have it known just how crude or rude or vulgar they can be. Look at that!" he pointed at Tomas' work.

"He wrote it all while we were away," David observed.

"I told you about time for us, David..."

"You said it didn't mean much to us," David said. "Maybe we were gone for years."

"I always felt death coming on in the fall," Hemingway said.

"And not on the front lines?"

"There, too," Hemingway agreed. "And I could always write up a storm until I found myself in a winter with no end to it. I should have pinched the woman on the ass. It's been so long since I touched a woman..."

"Don't look at me that way!" David warned, backing away from the chair.

"There's no evidence I was a homosexual," Hemingway reminded him.

"Are my lips like your friend's were?"

"They don't look Irish to me," Hemingway cackled. "I won't be kissing them. For your ears only, David, I preferred women. Some days, women look beautiful. Other days, they talk so much you can't look at them. A beautiful woman can be found anywhere. Good whiskey has to be made."

"You liked sex and alcohol," David said.

"You will, too," Hemingway said. "People who have committed suicide..."

"Go on," David urged when Hemingway paused.

273

"...are required to spend what was left of life imprisoned close to the earth. I became Catholic after my second marriage. For a Catholic, anyone committing suicide goes to Hell. But other religions are more tolerant, and, depending on which religion you want to believe--gone to Hell or imprisoned until that time passes then the spirit goes over somewhere to be damned, cursed, or redeemed—will make no difference to you. Now that is where you found me, though. I went to the trout stream, because that place where all like spirits dwell outside this house, and sometimes inside houses, is not a fun place to be. There are a lot of demons and low life scum in the wilderness of it. I once made the mistake of saying death was just another whore. It's worse! It's just that one real story that can't be written. I've figured out some of this..."

"This what?" David asked.

"This curse of you... It was an Italian author who wrote that what a writer creates would never die. Therefore, I am alive until my works die. You found me. I hope to hell none of my other characters come after me. Sometimes I feel one lurking about, but... You are the only creation of mine that I will not give the gift of death. I don't know how Tomas managed to write his words so quickly. It's like you in the book and I did when the suitcase disappeared, but I never expected it would happen to anyone else. I came back here to write an apology."

"What were you going to write?" David asked.

"This: I am truly—did you see that?"

"See what?" David asked.

"I wrote t-r-u-e-l-y," Hemingway said. "Watch me do it again!" Hemingway said typing: t-r-u-e-l-y. As soon as he hit the space bar the word changed, instantly corrected: truly. "See that! The damned thing is possessed. That's how he was able to get it done!"

Chapter Sixty

"Where are we?" David asked.

"We are at the end," Hemingway said, sitting in the shade near the river.

"The end?" David asked.

"And the beginning," Hemingway said. "Some call this place the cradle of civilization. No doubt it is one of several such places. Some have called this place Paradise, believing Eden was here with its Garden. I think it is time for me to write, don't you?"

"Write what?" David asked.

"What you have wanted me to write, David," Hemingway said, opening the notebook he held in his hand and taking a pencil from the wire binding. "As much as you want life, I've got to warn you again about it and that other thing you want me to give you..."

"What other thing?"

"Love," Hemingway shook his head as he placed the notebook on the ground. As he sharpened the pencil with the CASE XX of Tomas' that he carried in his pocket, he continued: "It's a good thing I was a believer in love at first sight. You want a woman like the second woman whose name we don't know...

Somehow that's fitting, but there is something perverse about love at first sight. It is powerful and poetic, but it is only a blind actress feeling her way by chance onto the stage of a play long in progress," and he laughed at his words.

David did not say anything. He could feel something, but he did not know whether he felt joy or hopelessness.

"I couldn't write well when I got the Nobel Prize in literature in 1954 for I was too sick. I didn't go to get the award. But what I wrote applies to what I'm about to write, David..."

"You're going to try something that has never been done...something others have tried but they couldn't do..."

"Damn! I should have known you would quote me. You got most of it right. This time it will take great luck to make your story real. That's the thrill of it though. Its like going back to the front lines in a war the way I did in May of 1944," he said, picking up the notebook and writing words that David could see...the ones he had waited for: **Much can come of it. The writing of it,**" Hemingway wrote. **David, when Saul tried to arm him with weaponry, used what he had always used, a stone. Standing before the Garden where God, himself, is absent for the moment, doing his own work which is no longer being written, David sees the cherub with the flaming sword...**

"What is that thing?" David asks, pointing toward the cherub.

"Protestant scholars would say it is only a symbolic representation of the abstract idea of an angel." Hemingway laughed. "Just be thankful that I chose not to write Ezekiel's vision of the Cherubim, with bodies of men, yet with four faces each. Imagine a cherub with a human face in front, like the sentry over there, but with an eagle's face behind and a lion's face to the left and an ox's face to the right. You can read the rest of his picturing of them later."

"Later?" David asked.

"When you are alive!" Hemingway said. "The cherub with its flaming sword is there to keep man from returning to the Garden, son, and eating of the fruit of the Tree of Life and becoming immortal like God. I'm here to write like God. I got this idea on the bus in Cleveland when I realized no one could see you except for me or me except for Tomas. I am going to delve into painful truths again as I always did in my work. That thing is there to keep man out of the Garden, and probably a man's spirit, but you are neither."

"I am nothing," David lamented.

"You are a writer! That was what I made you. You had no say in the matter, but you'll have to work at that part. A writer is not born. I will write you into the Garden, and the fruit can give you life, but I can't be alive for you, nor can you be alive for me after I do this."

"Won't that make you happy…"

"It will be my best work," Hemingway said, "but you'll be the only reader of it."

"Why do I have this sling and this stone?" David asked.

"There is possibly a tragedy in all of this," Hemingway laughed. "If I treat the cherub as though it is a bull and I a matador and if my thinking is correct and you are be able to enter the Garden unseen and eat the Forbidden Fruit, there will be no tragedy. So you will know which of the two trees is which, I will write the Tree of Life on the left. It may sound childish to tell you all these details since you will do everything exactly as I write it, but so you can have a clue about what lies ahead of you I'm going to write the serpent in the Tree of the Knowledge of Good and Evil. I will write the trees in the middle of the Garden the way they were before the Fall when God said: *Don't eat that fruit! Don't even touch* it!"

"What about this sling?" David asked, holding it up with his right hand.

"If I'm wrong," Hemingway said, "and it does see you, hurl that stone better than you did when you tried to hit the squirrel with that slingshot and get the hell out of here…"

Chapter Sixty-one

David kept his eyes closed, reading the words as they were written: **It was nearly dark when David turned off the main road that ran beside the river. The road was empty. The sun had gone down. The cherub was a little cherub with a long flaming sword. If the thing went well, David would enter the garden. The thing went well, indeed. The cherub moved away from David onto the bare cleared space, and like Lot's wife David turned to watch. He watched only long enough to see the first charge, an unsuccessful attempt to gore the matador. David remembered that in a real story, the matador never gets killed. He turned around and entered the garden. He made his way to the middle of it. And David ate of the fruit of the Tree of Life and then started to walk toward the woman who was ravishing, but returned to the Tree of Life to pick another fruit. He rushed toward the naked woman who held the fruit of the Tree of the Knowledge of Good and Evil in her hand and when he tasted her fruit... the serpent in the tree, wisest of all God's creatures said...**

David wanted to scream, but he did not. The pain he thought: *Why does it hurt so much. I can't stand...*

He squinted and with his eyes closed tighter saw words—for a moment saw Tomas typing: **I finished the novel. It took on a life of its own the way a story does. I'll leave it for you with your present...**

Try as he could, David saw no more words. They were gone.

"Run! Run!" the woman yelled. "Let's get out of here—now!"

David opened his eyes.

"It's good to see those baby blues of yours," the nurse said to David as the chopper's blades, flaming through the burning sun, churned up sand and dust near the landing pad. "We'll get you out of the Sunni Triangle as soon as they load your buddy."

"Where's Papa," David asked, wondering: *Are my eyes blue?*"

"That's odd," the nurse said. "In that bumpy ride in the back of the ambulance from your Humvee here, your buddy asked the same question."

The ambulance driver, shaking his head, another marine and the pilots positioned the stretcher with the second marine onto the helicopter. The nurse covered the man's bloody, swollen face.

"I'm sorry," she said. "He didn't make it. We'll take you from here to an air-conditioned tent where a surgeon will take care of those legs. In the morning, you'll be on your way to Landstuhl Army Medical Center in Germany."

"What happened?" David asked.

"You don't remember?"

"No," David said.

"Nick said..."

"Nick who?" David asked.

"Your buddy," she said, pointing, "there on the stretcher. He said you were trying to drive around the Humvee in front of you after it was hit. He said the next thing he remembered there was a boom and life changed..."

"His story had gone on long enough," David said.

"What?"

"Nothing," David said. "There was a snake...in the tree...with legs...and..."

"I know it's hard to be clear headed in a time like this. You are gravely wounded, but it's good to hear you talk," the nurse said. "Dust, smoke and shrapnel are what I deal with every day. Back home nobody realizes how these insurgents target ambulances with their secondary bombs timed to strike us when we come to help the injured. Are you in a lot of pain?"

"Yes," David said his body convulsing.

"What I'm going to do," she said as the chopper left the landing pad, "is insert a catheter linked to this painkiller dispenser that you can operate by hand. This is a procedure we've perfected on the battlefield for the first time during this campaign. It allows you to be conscious and in control while disabling only the nerves that produce your pain. We're kind of pushing the science right now. War tends to call for desperate measures..."

When she finished the procedure, she wiped David's forehead.

"Thanks," he said.

"How long have you been an ambulance driver?" she asked.

"I can't remember," David said.

"Don't worry," she said. "Retrograde amnesia, the total blackout of memory that soap opera writers love to script, is rare. It'll come back to you."

"Did you ever send Tomas a poem?" David asked.

"Tomas who?"

"The writer in Kentucky," David answered, his pain gone.

"Are you from Kentucky?"

"I don't think so," David said.

"Nick said he followed you and Papa here from Kentucky. Said he followed the two of you from an A-frame there. Was Papa the gunner on the Humvee ahead of you?"

"A ghost," David said.

"Yes," she said. "He died, too. I'm sorry we didn't know in time to bring his body along. Had we known it, we would have, the three of you being so close…"

"Nick wasn't there, but you were…"

"Then I'm the one with amnesia," she laughed. "When my memory comes back, I'll send him a poem."

"You need to," David said.

"All you have to do now," she said, putting the dispenser in his left hand and squeezing his fingers, "is pump this like that until the pain goes away."

"Whew!" David sighed, pumping rapidly. "That's good stuff."

"Thank you, sir," she laughed. "I've got to confess. You are my first. If I haven't found the right nerves, I'll have to do the procedure again. I'm sure I've pinpointed them. If I have, I can adjust the flow..."

"You're beautiful..."

"You're not the first wounded soldier to tell me that," she said. "I'm not an angel..."

"You have an angel's smile. I love you and I'm going to marry you," he said. "We'll go to Spain on our honeymoon."

"Now that's original," she laughed.

"Have I asked you your name?"

David looked into her eyes after he asked, and when she smiled, the memory of her from that first time when she sat in front of the computer reading while Tomas read her eyes—while he lay silent beneath the bed—that memory returned. He realized it had pursued him unceasingly. He had never loved, but now he knew he had to love her or hate her. Whatever he felt for her, be it desire that possessed his mind brought on by the thrill of seeing her up close for the first time or... Pain shot through him and he remembered the second fruit that Papa had him pick. Papa was wrong. He had not forgotten him. The man lived inside him…"

"No, you've haven't asked" she said. "My name is Catherine…"

"Do you want a bite of this, Catherine?" David asked, holding up his right arm while he pumped painkiller into the nerves in his legs with the fingers of his left hand.

"No," Catherine laughed again as she looked at his empty hand. "I think you'd better slow down on that painkiller. You mustn't put yourself into a coma."